ADVANCE PRAISE FOR
The Kid from Dodgertown

"Dodgertown was a dream come true for my grandfather. He had envisioned a place that would serve as a training foundation for a Brooklyn Dodger dynasty. But this training base surprisingly became something beyond that, transcending into a realm where not only players' talents were honed, but a place where lasting bonds formed, commitment and dedication were shaped, and where, steadily, proud histories evolved, all imbued with the magic of that common nucleus, a magic conveyed in Mr. Ferrante's telling of the tale."
-Branch B. Rickey, 3rd generation baseball executive

"It brought me great joy to read that my father, Joe Black, is one of the Brooklyn Dodger heroes in this tale, where opportunities and dreams come true. Welcome to Dodgertown!"
-Martha Jo Black, Chicago White Sox

"I came to Dodgertown as a rookie broadcaster in 1950 and never missed a game there until the Dodgers left in 2008… and I left a piece of my heart there as well. This book will take you for a stroll through a very special place."
-Vin Scully, Hall of Fame broadcaster

"The one constant over 60 years of Dodger Baseball History was Dodgertown in Vero Beach. I trained there as a player and went back many times afterwards. It's wonderful that someone is keeping the memory of Dodgertown alive."
-Carl Erskine, Brooklyn Dodger great

ALSO BY PAUL FERRANTE

Young Adult
The T.J. Jackson Mysteries (Fire and Ice Books)
Last Ghost at Gettysburg
Spirits of the Pirate House
Roberto's Return
Curse of the Fairfield Witch
The Voodoo Cult's Treasure
Terror in the Tower

* * *

30 Minutes in Memphis: A Beatles Story (The Ionian
Press)
The Girl Who Stole J.E.B. Stuart (The Ionian Press)
The Kid from Dodgertown (The Ionian Press)

Adult

The Rovers: A Tale of Fenway (Melange Books)
A Bermuda Triangle Love Story (The Ionian Press)

PAUL FERRANTE

The Ionian Press

Print ISBN: 978-1-7324857-8-5

For all those like me
Who believe in the magic of Baseball

THE KID FROM DODGERTOWN

Chapter One
Late January, 2021

Rosa Santos settled into her customary second row center seat in the Dodger Stadium press room and yawned as activity buzzed around her. She'd received a text the previous day that the Dodgers had signed relief pitcher Darnell "Heater" Hayward to bolster their bullpen as they prepared to defend their 2020 World Series championship. She was the Dodgers' beat reporter for *El Comentario*, one of the largest Hispanic newspapers in Los Angeles, and one of the most respected in America; therefore, it was her duty to be in attendance for the presser announcing Hayward's signing. So, she'd schlepped from her condo on the outskirts of LA, braving the columns of vehicles inching along the Freeway, until she reached the home of the reigning World Champs in Chavez Ravine.

As she awaited the beginning of the festivities, Rosa, a petite brunette with a café au lait complexion and expressive brown eyes that were somewhat obscured by her stylishly tinted glasses, discreetly scanned the room for others who might be staring at her.

This was not because she sought attention; far from it. It was because just a few months before, she had been at the center of a scandal that had forced the resignation of Jimmy "Bulldog" Barry, one of Major League Baseball's most popular young managers.

"Insta-gate," as it had come to be called on ESPN—and everywhere else, as a result—came about when Barry, the skipper of one of the American League's Central Division teams, took an interest in her during Spring Training of 2019 in Arizona. She was there, of course, covering the Dodgers, and first encountered Barry behind the backstop of the club's home ballpark prior to a preseason game. A harmless exchange of pleasantries, which included a compliment about her luxurious hair, was quickly forgotten—by her, anyway. Because Rosa knew that despite being unmarried, relationships with any baseball personnel while executing the duties of her job would be highly unprofessional and would compromise her credibility as a sports journalist. This was something she had worked hard to cultivate since her days as a stringer for a small paper in her native Dominican Republic. Rosa was rarely impressed with ballplayers anyway, because even though many of them were physically attractive, she found the younger ones to be maddeningly immature, and the older ones jaded and imbued with a strong sense of entitlement.

Besides, "Bulldog" was dribbling tobacco juice down the front of his jersey—part of his "colorful" image—and she couldn't imagine anything more repugnant than that… except maybe that the guy had a wife and two young kids back home and was clearly flirting with her.

However, in baseball circles, the former All-Star slugger had garnered positive attention during the past season by taking over a poor team and turning the franchise around, narrowly missing the playoffs in the current expanded post-season format. On top of that, he was regarded as a fiery, charismatic leader, and the media had warmed to him instantly. His antics, whether they entailed animatedly arguing with umpires or goofing around with regular fans even during the games, earned constant airtime for him on the nightly highlight shows. He was considered "a breath of fresh air" amid the current analytic robo-managers populating the Major Leagues. That was why what followed caused such an uproar, and nearly ruined Rosa Santos's life.

It started with text messages from Barry that suggested they meet for a drink and a chat—about baseball, of course. Then, despite her attempts to rebuff the creep, it escalated to where he was sending her suggestive shirtless photos of himself and asking for dates. The more she said no thanks, the more he pursued her, even after Spring Training had ended. An interleague series between his club and the Dodgers in July, set amid the chaotic backdrop of the Covid-19 pandemic, gave him an opportunity to redouble his efforts.

By this time, Rosa was exasperated and concerned. This guy, whose team was again fighting for the lead in their division, wouldn't take no for an answer. So, she was constantly harassed by him. But what to do? She knew that as an attractive woman, her voicing displeasure to the powers that be, whether that included her superiors at *El Comentario* or MLB, could blow up in her face and cause her to become the victim of reverse retribution. After all, who was going to take the word of a female Hispanic nobody over that of a wildly popular Gringo manager?

Finally, by season's end she'd had it. Thankfully, Barry's team had been eliminated in the new "play-in" game that initiated the post season, allowing him to return to his All-American family back East, but that didn't stop the texts, Instagrams, or now, phone messages left at all times of the day. At wits end, Rosa decided to act.

First, she spoke to her parents back in the Dominican, who listened cautiously to her story. When her father determined that Rosa's pleas of innocence in the matter were genuine, he hit the ceiling, threatening to track the American manager down and beat him senseless. Her mother, a more pragmatic, level-headed person, shrugged her shoulders and told Rosa that the career path she'd chosen, though admirable, was one that was not suitable for a young woman, especially a young, *unattached* woman. She had always wanted her daughter to give up the writing gig and settle down, and this situation, in her mind anyway, validated her beliefs. In short, Rosa's parents, though they loved and supported her, were no help at all.

Next up was Felipe Rodriguez, the sports editor for *El Comentario*. A father of girls himself, Rodriguez was sympathetic, listening intently as she told her story. "You have evidence?" he asked.

"Yes," said Rosa. "I saved all the texts, Instagram photos, everything."

Her boss sat back in his seat and closed his eyes for a few moments. Then he leaned forward, placed his elbows on his desk, and glared across it at her. "Rosa," he said, "what you've told me pains me deeply. You are a fine journalist with a lucrative career ahead of you. But I am afraid for you here.

"If we take the matter to this man's ballclub, and by extension, Major League Baseball, there will be repercussions. It becomes your word against his—"

"But I have evidence!" she blurted.

"I don't doubt that, Rosa," he said gently. "Or that you are completely in the right here. But are you willing to risk the notoriety you might receive by bringing this man's behavior to light? This isn't just your issue… it's a *societal* issue."

Rodriguez sat back again. "I want you to sleep on this tonight," he said measuredly, "and, if tomorrow you feel the need to proceed with bringing charges against this man, come see me and we will set things in motion. But if you don't, I will understand."

Rosa set her jaw. "There's nothing to sleep on," she said. "I want to go forward, if not for me, then for all the women like me in the media who are subjected to this kind of treatment."

And so, Rosa Santos's ordeal began.

Accompanied by Felipe Rodriguez and her lawyer, like her a Hispanic woman, Rosa approached Bulldog Barry's team's hierarchy. Predictably, they were aghast at the news, and then suspicious that the reporter was simply looking for fame, a payday, or both. But when her lawyer laid out the portfolio of evidence Rosa had accumulated, they had no choice but to bring their manager in to face the charges. Of course, he initially denied everything. In fact, Barry gambled on his status in MLB and decided, even when faced with Rosa's overwhelming evidence, to fight the accusations tooth and nail. Thus, the investigation was turned over to the internal affairs division of MLB, and the circus commenced.

Originally, it had been decided that Rosa was coming forward only under the condition of anonymity. Her lawyer promised to not publicize their accusations of the manager in any way, in return for MLB keeping her name out of it. This was easier said than done, because once word leaked out that the popular manager was under investigation for "conduct detrimental to the game" and that said conduct involved numerous unwanted advances to a female journalist, a media frenzy ensued, with pundits venturing ideas as to whom Barry's accuser might be.

To his credit, Barry, whose trophy wife stood stoically by his side, went along with the deal to keep Rosa's identity a secret. Nonetheless, after a few weeks of digging, there was no doubt the man had been caught red-handed, and he was indefinitely suspended by MLB. Of course, the fact that powerful women's rights groups had jumped on this case, threatening protests and boycotts of games of that manager and his team throughout the season, had helped seal his fate. This would be a real black eye for the game that it couldn't afford, not with sporadic incidents of domestic violence by its players that kept cropping up.

And so, it seemed that Rosa Santos's decision to shine the light on the despicable behavior of a Major League manager was the right one—that is, until the owner of Barry's team, in a momentous gaffe that was dubious at best, let her name slip in the press conference announcing the manager's release.

This screwup, which he passionately maintained was accidental, unleashed a torrent of publicity, both positive and negative, upon the journalist. She received hundreds of letters of support from women across the country who had been victims of discrimination, harassment, or abuse from men who got away with this behavior. Women's groups lauded her courage. Even Oprah and *60 Minutes* came calling for an interview, which she politely declined.

On the flipside, the journalist was subjected to

relentless hate mail from fans of the fired manager's team, as well as chauvinistic men in general, who characterized her as either a publicity-seeking gold digger, though no financial restitution was ever asked for or delivered, or an outright floozy.

Gradually, things calmed down during the 2020 season, when the worldwide pandemic pushed her name off the sports pages. Rosa simply went back to work covering the Dodgers, though she noticed a marked hesitancy in most MLB personnel to interact with her in any manner. To his credit, Felipe Rodriguez stood by her, telling the woman that the position at *El Comentario* was hers as long as she wanted it, which was a comfort. Hey, with her enormous condo rent and car payments, she *had* to hold onto this job. She didn't know anything else.

But the whole sordid affair had soured her on baseball, a game she had loved since joining the local boys back in the Dominican for spirited sandlot games where milk cartons were fashioned into gloves, broomsticks served as bats, and wads of friction tape passed for baseballs. Now she viewed it as a cutthroat business, where the bottom line had replaced the joy of what she had once considered the perfect game

And so it was with jaded boredom that Rosa flipped through the notes that had been handed out to all attending media on the background of the Dodgers' newest hired gun.

* * *

According to the club's PR department, right-hander Darnell Hayward, known by his nickname "Heater," age twenty-six, was signed by his hometown Kansas City

Royals in 2015 after two seasons of junior college ball. After a rapid rise through the Royals' farm system, he'd made the big club in 2018 and had amassed an impressive 2.36 ERA (with a 0.90 WHP) in three seasons with Kansas City. But then, despite what seemed to be an ideal situation with his wife and young daughter comfortably ensconced in the suburbs of his hometown, he had opted for free agency with the expressed desire of signing with the Los Angeles Dodgers. This declaration, of course, eliminated much of the leverage he could have applied on the free-agent market, and Rosa found this strange, in an era where players' agents squeezed every dime they could get out of MLB teams in contract negotiations. Besides, the Dodgers were coming off a World Series win and were loaded talent-wise. Where would he fit in? And did this Midwestern kid realize that LA-LA land and Kansas City were worlds apart?

She was turning these ideas over and jotting down notes in the margins of the press release when Dodgers president of baseball operations Andrew Friedman and manager Dave Roberts led the young man onto the dais, followed by his pretty wife and adorable daughter, so he could meet the media.

The Dodgers' new relief pitcher was much darker than Rosa, with his hair shorn close to the scalp and piercing eyes. She judged him to be slightly shorter than his 6'2" listing, with broad shoulders and a lean build. Of course, the billowy Dodgers jersey that was draped over his shirt and tie obscured any definition to his frame. He got comfortable as Friedman introduced him, followed by the official welcome from manager Roberts, with whom Rosa had always maintained a relationship of mutual respect. She noticed a reserved calm about Hayward, whose broad smile seemed genuine—though she had yet to see a new free agent signee display anything less. After he finished, Roberts nodded to his new pitcher, who cleared his throat and spoke:

"Hello, everybody. As you know, I'm Darnell Hayward, and this is my wife Tami and my daughter Jacqui," he began, flashing a 100-watt smile. "All I can say is, I'm just so happy to be a part of the Dodger family. It's a team with a great tradition, and becoming a part of it is a dream come true. So, I'll answer any questions you have." They came fast and furious as cameras whirred and writers scribbled:

"What number will you be wearing?"

"Well, I've worn #49 since my senior year of high school, but as you know, that number's been taken by Blake Treiner, who's a really good pitcher, so number 49's on lockdown."

There were chuckles all around, and Rosa nodded her approval of Hayward's acknowledgment of his place as a new recruit. Most players today had little respect for baseball's traditions, or even cared.

"Of course," he went on, "my next idea was to reverse it, and I think that might be a solution."

"Why 49?" asked a reporter from MLB Network. "Any significance to it?"

"It's kind of a personal thing," he said. "It's Blake's number and let's leave it at that."

"You had a great thing going in Kansas City. What do you think about LA so far?"

"I love the palm trees," he said with a grin. "Seriously, though, it's different from Kansas City, no doubt. But I'll adjust. It's worth it to play for the Dodgers."

Rosa raised her hand, and he nodded in her direction.

"As a free agent coming off a great season, you could have played the free agency field more, as many teams are in need of relief pitchers. Why did you declare your desire to come here so early in the game?"

"It's a long story, Ms. Santos," he said respectfully as he held her gaze, which prompted some raised eyebrows in the room over his acknowledgment of her identity. "I wouldn't want to bore everyone here. All I can say is, this is where I was destined to be, and Mr. Roberts, my teammates, and the entire Dodger organization and its fans will get my very best, every time I go out there."

From there, the presser meandered a bit, with Hayward being asked about his pitching repertoire ("Fastball, curve, occasional changeup") and preference as to his relief role ("Anytime in the game Mr. Roberts wants to use me") and his reported involvement in the community ("Tami and I started a program back in Kansas City to get more African American kids involved in baseball, and we intend to keep our off-season residence there and stick with it. Kansas City is where I grew up, and where my family and heart will always be. I'm sure you can relate to that"). When a reporter asked about his laid-back demeanor, Dave Roberts interjected with, "Yeah? Just try facing him in a clutch situation. He doesn't give an inch."

Shortly thereafter the presser ended, the media having gotten all the soundbites they needed for the six o'clock news. As her colleagues repaired to the buffet that the Dodgers had laid out for them or followed Hayward out of the building to the playing field for his obligatory photo op, Rosie yawned yet again and closed her notebook. Truth be told, there was nothing overly impressive about the Dodgers' new relief pitcher. He gave all the pat answers and employed most of the clichés new players used ad nauseum. "Dream come true" was the one that really made Rosa grind her teeth. Perhaps the whole Insta-gate deal over the past year had irreparably tainted her view of the game she used to love so passionately. And perhaps her malaise was so obvious that Hayward had noticed, because as she was on her way out, a young member of the Dodgers' PR staff was tapping her on the shoulder. "Yes, what?" she said curtly.

"Ms. Santos," he said nervously, "Mr. Hayward wondered if he could have a word with you after he gets finished with the photos out on the field?"

"Okay, whatever." She grabbed a turkey sandwich and a bottle of seltzer and wandered out to the brilliant sunshine as the Dodgers' team photographers and assorted media snapped photos of Hayward, with and without his family and Dave Roberts. Rosa waited in the Dodger dugout, munching her sandwich and glancing at her watch, until the photo op had run its course and the people dispersed. After shaking hands with his new manager and sending his wife and daughter inside for some lunch, the pitcher ambled over to the dugout, removing his Dodgers jersey and loosening his tie as he went.

"Hi," he said, sitting down next to her. "Good sandwich?"

"Too much mayo," she answered, wiping a bit of the white stuff from the corner of her mouth. "So, what can I do for you?"

"Well," he said, "for starters you can lose the attitude. I'm not the enemy, Rosa." He said this so calmly, so pleasantly, that she was not offended he'd called her by her first name.

"Well, okay then, *Darnell*," she replied. "Again, what is it that I can do for you before I melt in this dugout?"

He smiled. "Listen," he said. "I saw what you went through last year. I'm sorry it happened. I found the reaction of MLB, and the males in the media, disgusting. And I admired how you held up through it all, how you carried yourself."

"Thank you," she said. "It wasn't easy. It still isn't."

"I could see that today… the sideways glances you were getting from some of the others, for example."

"Yeah, well, that's baseball, I guess," she replied, crumpling her napkin into a golf ball.

"Not necessarily," he said, looking out at the field. "Not for me, anyway."

"Easy for you to say," she snapped. "What are they paying you this year… 1.8 mil or something?"

"That's not it," he said quietly. "There's more to it."

"*Sure* there is, Darnell," she countered. "Like when you said coming here was your dream and your destiny. C'mon, man."

He turned and looked at her, and in his eyes was a sweet sadness she didn't expect to see. "You've been given a raw deal," he said. "I get that. But I think down deep you really love the game, or you wouldn't still be here."

"And how would you know this, Dr. Phil?"

"Because there was a time in my life when I was just like you. Even worse."

"You don't say."

"I *do* say. And I'd like you to be the one that I tell this story to."

"Why me?"

"Because you could use it."

"Oh, really? How do you know what I need?"

He closed his eyes and regrouped. "Maybe I said it wrong. What I mean is, I have a story to tell that I think some people would have a hard time understanding."

"But I won't?"

"That's my hope. I've had it inside me a long time. But when I learned about what you went through, I felt we had a lot in common. And I hoped even more that the Dodgers would sign me, so I—we—could share this."

"Should I say I'm honored?" For the first time, she betrayed the hint of a smile.

"I don't know about that," he replied. "But I think you'll be interested. There's just one catch."

"And that is?"

"You can't tell it until I retire."

"*What!*"

"I mean it. If you do, they'll think I'm crazy, and that you're even crazier. Trust me on this. When we're done it will all be worth it. Even if you never print a word of it."

Rosa, intrigued, squinted an eye. "Does your wife know about the story?" she asked.

"Nobody in my family knows. Nobody in *this world* knows, for that matter."

She thought for a moment. "Okay, deal," she said. "I hope this tale of yours lives up to the hype."

"It's a long story, Rosa," he said with a reassuring smile. "But it's a good story."

* * *

For the next five months, the journalist and the ballplayer met in out-of-the-way places during Spring

Training in Arizona, and in LA and various other cities once the season started. They were always discreet, and nobody ever knew that the journalist and the ball player were collaborating, not even Hayward's family. By the time it was over, Rosa Santos had filled a handful of cassette tapes and two notebooks with information. What follows is what he told her.

Chapter Two
Winter, 2012

I never wanted to go to Florida. You might think that's strange, because April in Kansas City is usually cold and rainy, with a stray snowstorm thrown in. To not want to see palm trees swaying in the warm breeze defies all logic. But the thing is, I wasn't going to Florida for the beach—I was going there to play baseball, and I hated it.

So then you might ask, why would you hate the game that could make you wealthy and famous? Well, that's a story that goes back to when I was a kid coming up in Kansas City.

You see, my grandpa, Willie Jackson, played in the Negro Leagues for the Kansas City Monarchs in the early '50s and had even been in the minors with the Brooklyn Dodgers. After that, he settled down and had a job for years and years with the Kansas City recreation department. After my grandmother died, he went to live with his daughter, who's my mom, and my dad. Both of them are long time teachers at a local junior college, where they met. My folks were also involved in athletics; Dad played basketball in high school, and Mom was a track star right through college at Missouri. So, as you can imagine, I inherited some crazy good athletic genes. But nobody, not even my grandpa, ever pushed me to play sports. In fact, he hardly ever talked about his career as a ballplayer. I got the impression that it hadn't ended well, but figured it was personal, and if he really wanted to tell me about it, he would.

Despite all this, I signed up for Little League and found out pretty quickly that I was way better than the other kids. I've always been a good line drive hitter, but it was as a pitcher that I got the coaches' attention right from the start. I could throw hard without exerting myself too much, and I could keep the ball around the plate. More importantly, I could throw two or three times a week with no problem. So, year after year I was the ace of my team's pitching staff, right through Little League and Babe Ruth League and Cal Ripken League.

When I got to high school at KC South, Coach Crockett on the varsity had already seen me pitch quite a few times and had even talked to my parents about my potential. He told them I'd be on the varsity by my sophomore year, if not sooner, with the right tutelage. Which they thought was all well and good, as long as I put my schoolwork first. And I did, maintaining a B+ average throughout.

As Coach Crockett predicted, I was one of the Kansas City South Falcons' starters by my soph year, playing the outfield when I wasn't pitching so they could get my bat in the lineup. Then, as a junior, I started the season 3-0, with an ERA under two and a lot of strikeouts. I was hitting the low 90s on the radar gun, too. College scouts were starting to show up at our games, and they were easy to spot because hardly anyone came out to see baseball at our school. KC South was foremost a football school, for one thing; and also, the weather was usually lousy until late in the season, when nature would flip a switch and Kansas City would turn into a furnace. That's why the whole Florida thing came about, but more on that later. First, I've gotta tell you how my high school career came crashing down.

It started out innocently enough. We were playing Rockhurst, and it was a bright, sunny day for a change. Rockhurst had a reputation for being patient at the plate, but that shouldn't have mattered. I mean, I'd shut them down the previous year when I was only a sophomore. So, like usual, I blew through the first inning, striking out the side. I was even thinking no-hitter. Can you believe that? But then the roof fell in. I walked the leadoff man of the second inning. No big deal, right?

Then I walked the next guy.

And the next guy.

And it's not like I was a little off the plate; my catcher, Paco Gonzalez, had to dive for some of my pitches like a hockey goalie. When the bases were loaded, Coach Crockett motioned for Paco to go out to the mound and settle me down. So, he called time, tipped his mask back on his helmet, and jogged out.

"*Que pasa,* Darnell?" he said between spits. "You hurt or somethin'?"

"Nope," I said, looking over his shoulder—Paco was built like a fireplug—into the mostly empty stands.

"Then what's the deal? You're not even comin' close, bro."

"I don't know," I said. Because I really didn't.

So Paco turned toward Coach Crockett and shrugged his shoulders, as if to say, "Don't ask me." Which prompted Crockett to sprint out to the mound himself. And we went through the whole process all over again.

"You hurt?"

"No, Coach."

"Is the mound okay?"

"It's fine."

"Is the ball too slick? Your grip is good?"

"Yup."

He and Paco looked at each other and shrugged. So, he patted me on the butt, said, "Then let's go get 'em," and ran back to the dugout. Paco got back behind the plate, pounded his glove, and squatted. "Let's go, Darnell!" he grunted.

I nodded, and then promptly hit the next batter in the knee. One run scored.

Then I threw a pitch that narrowly missed the following batter's head. Another run in.

When I sailed my next pitch three feet over the next batter's head, Crockett was right back on the mound, this time to take me out. "Not your day, big guy," he said as I handed him the ball. "We'll work on this tomorrow. No big thing."

But he was wrong. Because no matter how much Coach Crockett or our pitching coach, Mr. Putney, who also taught physics at KC South, tried to work with me, I just got worse. We tried everything—watching tons of video of me throwing, going to a no-windup motion, having me stand to the right or left of the pitching rubber. Nothing worked. And when Putney started applying rules of physics to my throwing motion, it screwed me up even more.

So, by midseason I was done as a starting pitcher, never mind being the ace of the staff. And without a number one starter, we quickly fell out of contention for the sectional playoffs. Of course, I could still play the outfield, but I started to feel like I was stealing someone else's position because I couldn't pitch. And even more, the wildness thing started affecting my hitting, too, because I was always thinking about it. By season's end, I just wanted it to be over. I was tired of the looks of pity I got from my teammates; the whispers around school of how I'd just "lost it." The snide remarks of some kids who reveled in the idea of my college scholarship or getting signed by a Major League team going out the window.

Did it have anything to do with my being black? I don't think so, though I was the only black kid on the team. It was more of a general jealousy thing, I think. Plus, the fact that I wasn't a big socializer or partier. I got along with everybody, including my teachers, but nobody really knew me. I was kind of a mystery, so the other kids kept their distance.

My parents tried to sympathize with me, keep me from despairing, even telling me that if I never played another baseball game it was fine with them. But it ate me up. Today they call me "Heater," but by that summer I was known at South as "Head Case," and it was well deserved. I was a mess.

Somehow I got talked into playing American Legion ball, with the manager, an older guy who was good friends with Coach Crockett, assuring me that I'd only play the outfield, but I was so miserable that I quit by midsummer, somehow convincing myself that a prolonged vacation from baseball would be the cure for my wildness problems, and that I'd come back for my senior season with a fresh perspective and be ready to get after it. But I was just kidding myself.

What made it even worse, if that was possible, is that someone slipped the photocopy of a Wikipedia article into my school locker about this guy named Steve Blass. Ever heard of him?

Steve Blass was a right-handed pitcher for the Pittsburgh Pirates way back in the 1960s and '70s. He was pretty good, too. In 1969 he won sixteen games with lots of strikeouts, and by 1972 he had over a hundred wins and had made the National League All-Star Team. He'd even won two games for the Pirates in the '71 World Series, including the deciding 7th game. So the guy was clutch. But then, in 1973, he suddenly lost it. Couldn't throw strikes if his life depended on it. After trying everything, both physical and mental, to snap out of it, he just gave up. By '74 he was done. So, some genius called his situation, condition, whatever, "Steve Blass disease," and the name stuck.

No matter what the cause of his "disease," Blass never regained his ability to throw strikes. He later went on to have a successful career as a Pirates broadcaster, but you have to believe that everyone around him was wondering what might have been, and if he was just a head case.

Like me.

Then, more recently, there was Rick Ankiel, who went through the same thing as Blass in 2000. This guy came to the Majors with the St. Louis Cardinals throwing in the high 90s, *serious gas*, but he had a wicked curveball, too. He even came in second in the voting for National League Rookie of the Year.

But in the 2000 National League Division Championship Series, after he breezed through the first couple innings of Game One, he just plain lost it. *On national TV*. He allowed—get this—four runs on a couple of hits, a bunch of walks, and *five wild pitches* before being pulled. He tried to shrug it off (sound familiar?), but when the Cardinals started him in the next round of the playoffs against the New York Mets, he imploded again and got yanked. The Cards pitched him in relief later in that series, which they lost, but he didn't do any better. Of course, the media started saying he had Steve Blass Disease.

Long story short, Rick reinvented himself as an outfielder, and three years later made it all the way back to the Show, where he had success with the Cardinals and some other teams. He even hit 25 homers one season, and had a real gun in the outfield, throwing out lots of guys on the basepaths. He still had that great arm, see what I'm saying? I guess that's why Coach Crockett, through a mutual acquaintance, had Rick give me a call.

By 2011 Rick's career was winding down, with injuries suffered by crashing into outfield walls and whatnot taking their toll. But he couldn't have been nicer when he talked to me. He asked me to tell him my side of the story, and really listened while I described what I'd been going through since that day versus Rockhurst. And although he was a lefty, I decided we were very much alike. In the end, though, although he didn't shut the door on me ever pitching again, he did remind me that, like him, I had a rifle arm, and that playing the outfield wasn't the worst thing in the world. I thanked him for his time and hung up, still as confused as ever.

Which brings us to the Florida trip.

Coach Crockett had been at KC South for five years by now, and he was sick of the terrible weather and muddy fields we had to deal with each spring. So, he came up with this idea to stage a fundraiser through the Varsity Booster Club to send our team down to Florida for a week. And since the parents of a couple of my teammates were well off, they had no problem getting their wealthy friends to contribute to the cause. Also, Coach had heard that the facility where the Dodgers used to have Spring Training, in a town called Vero Beach, was available for high school and college teams to come down and train. So, on a whim, Coach called down there and ended up talking to a guy in the front office named Joe Burgos, who he'd played college ball with. And it just so happened that Historic Dodgertown, as it was now called, had space available for a team after another one had backed out. We'd even get a reduced rate, because the first team had lost their deposit. When Crockett heard that, he jumped on it, even though we hadn't even reached the fundraiser's goal yet.

As you can imagine, the guys on the team went wild. I mean, Florida in April? That's a no-brainer. Who wouldn't want a chance to play baseball in the warmth of the Sunshine State?

Darnell "Head Case" Hayward, that's who.

Because once we started our winter workouts in the fieldhouse at South, it was pretty clear that despite my time away from the game, and Rick Ankiel's words of encouragement, I was just as clueless as to what was wrong with me as I'd been the previous season. But still, Coach was determined to get me right again. Part of this was that his personality is one that just doesn't accept defeat, at least not without a fight. And also because our team was short on pitchers, and, if we were to have any shot at all at the sectionals this season, I'd have to play a role—maybe not as the ace of the staff, but as a reliable arm in the rotation.

Unfortunately, this added pressure made things even

worse. I started having nightmares of meltdowns in big games. I even had one where my arm just broke off at the shoulder and went flying towards home plate! No joke. I'd wake up in a cold sweat from these dreams and dreaded going to the winter workouts.

And if that wasn't bad enough, my girlfriend dumped me. Vanessa Tyson and I had started going together my junior year before I got the "disease." She was really cute, though not exactly a rocket scientist. Still, we had a lot of fun together. We both enjoyed hip-hop music and movies, and I guess she liked the idea of being the girlfriend of a hotshot pitching prospect; a couple of times she had even hinted at us getting married down the road, though I definitely wasn't up for that. Talk about pressure!

Anyway, that problem was easily solved one day in February when I got home from practice and found a text—*a text*—on my phone telling me she thought we should try seeing other people, to "find out if we missed each other." For real. In other words, "Hit the road, Hayward."

That was the last straw. I was ready to go into school the next day and tell Coach Crockett I was quitting when I got a talking-to from my grandpa. By that time he was living with my parents, as my grandma had died of cancer the previous year. He said my mom had told him, because I was too afraid to, that I wasn't enjoying baseball anymore. And so, in his own way, he kind of advised me not to give up just yet. Well, how could I then tell him I was going into my coach's office the next day to hand in my stuff?

And then he said, in this dreamy voice, "I think you'll really like Dodgertown, Darnell. It's… kind of a special place."

"They call it 'Historic Dodgertown' now, PawPaw," I said, stupidly correcting him.

"They can call it anything they want, boy," he snapped. "To me it'll always be Dodgertown. And like I said, it's special. Maybe even magical."

"Magical how, PawPaw?" I asked.

"Cain't put my finger on it," he said, "and I was only there once, you understand, but you'll just have to see for yourself. Besides, you'll get out of this God-awful weather, and only a *fool* would pass up a week in Florida to stay in Kansas City."

And that's how I ended up in Dodgertown.

Chapter Three
April, 2012
Day One

Okay, so let me tell you a little more about Coach Crockett. He was definitely what you call "old-school." The analytics they use today in baseball had no value to him whatsoever. He went with his gut, and Coach's baseball instincts were usually correct. Now, as far as his personality, he wasn't exactly a nice guy—far from it. Coach would give you a good chewing out if the situation called for it; and with a bunch of high school hotshots to deal with, the situations were many. I mean, just his appearance—the graying crewcut, the tanned leathery face from years on the ballfield, the Popeye-like forearms, told you right away he was not to be messed with. By the time he coached me, he'd heard and seen it all. And even though he'd never been drafted by a Major League team, he'd put together a solid college career and had lots of connections in baseball. That's how we got to Dodgertown, remember.

One thing I admired about Coach was that he truly didn't see color. He treated me and Paco, who was our only Latino, the same as everyone else. Which meant we got chewed out like everyone else. But he also had a compassionate side. I mean, he really tried to help me get through my tough times, though what was going on was way out of his league.

On the other hand, our pitching coach, Mr. Putney, was all about technique and strategy; like I told you, he was by day a physics teacher. Even with his baseball uniform on, he looked like a physics teacher. His playing career hadn't got past Little League. He just loved baseball. Anyway, as a physics guy, Putney figured there was a logical explanation for everything that happened on a ballfield… including my pitching problems, of course. That's why I frustrated the heck out of him.

Oh, and one more thing about Coach Crockett. His favorite saying was, "Respect the game." For us that meant no hot-dogging or taunting on the field, no bat-flipping, no pointing to the sky after a big hit, and most of all, no excuse for not getting yourself in the best physical and mental state for every game. So while we did have some guys on the team who drank and smoked a little weed, they kept it under wraps, afraid to disappoint Coach. I wasn't big into that stuff, but there are few secrets on any team.

It's a lot different in the pros, of course. Guys are forever going out to clubs and other nonsense and doing stupid stuff, even the married guys, especially on the road. And I'm not being critical of them; I'm a live-and-let live person. But on our varsity team in 2012, you had to dress appropriately, even during the day at school; keep your average above a C+; and stay out of trouble, or Crockett would be on your butt in a nanosecond. I'm older now, but a lot of those old ways rubbed off on me, I guess.

The one thing Coach *couldn't* get some of us to do, though, was learn about and appreciate the history of the game. And that included me. Oh yeah, I knew who Babe

Ruth was, and Jackie Robinson and Roberto Clemente, but they were kinda like guys on old baseball cards to me. And the one person who could've schooled me on this stuff, my grandfather, never really went into his past, like I told you before. So, even though I'd heard about the Brooklyn Dodgers, I knew squat about their legacy, or about this Dodgertown place we were about to visit. And, truthfully, I was so wrapped up in my own issues that I didn't have time for it.

Maybe that's why Crockett came down the aisle on the plane before takeoff, handing out Wiki printouts on the history of Dodgertown for us to read during the flight. Of course, most of the guys just wanted to watch the on-board TV or play video games on their phones, but a few (not including me) did take the time to look it over. My seatmate, Paco, was one of them.

"Hey, Bro, check this out," he said. "The Dodgers built this training camp on the site of an old World War II air station. The first few years the players lived in barracks, like soldiers."

"Jeez, why would the team want to do that?" I said.

"Well, Bro, you might find this interesting. It's 'cause they had Jackie Robinson and a couple other black guys on the team, but the town where the base was, Vero Beach, was segregated. No blacks allowed in movie theaters, swimming pools, restaurants, you name it. But it wasn't just Vero Beach, man. *All* of Florida was like that. So the man who ran the Dodgers, that Branch Rickey guy who signed Robinson, decided the team needed a self-contained facility where the blacks and whites could room together, eat together, the whole nine. They even put in their own pool, tennis courts, golf course, and movie theater so the players never had to leave the place.

It was all about team bonding. So Dodgertown was ahead of its time. In fact, it says here that Dodgertown is the only athletic facility that's considered a Civil Rights Movement historical landmark. Anyway, the team stayed there all the way through 2008, when they moved their Spring Training headquarters to Arizona."

"Uh-huh," I said, as I was caught up in a mean game of Candy Crush on my cell phone.

Looking back, I should've paid more attention to what Paco was telling me. You know, he wasn't the most scholarly guy in the world—though behind the plate he was a great field general—but he obviously saw the significance of a couple minority players, namely us, going to stay in this historic place. And we would be rooming together, no less. Which was fine with me. Of all the guys on the team, Paco—who bore a strong resemblance to the Hall of Fame catcher Pudge Rodriguez—seemed to understand and like me the best. Maybe it was because we were the only minority guys on the team, I don't know. But maybe also because a pitcher and his catcher develop a special bond. They've got to be on the same page mentally or you'll have a disaster on your hands. I like to think I had the closest relationship with him of all the pitchers on the squad. The other guys probably either underestimated Paco's intelligence, or maybe were a bit racist. Especially this one guy, Trey Knight, who'd replaced me as the ace of the staff and was a real pain in the butt. But I'll get to him later.

So anyway, we settled into our seats after takeoff, and since it was an early-morning flight out of Kansas City, some guys fell asleep right away. Like I said, others watched TV or did some phone stuff, or read Coach's history sheets. But after awhile I found myself just staring out the window, wondering what lay ahead, as the Midwest cornfields faded away behind the clouds.

One more thing about that flight. We went no-frills coach out of Kansas City, which is all we could afford. Now that I've been in The Show for a few years, flying is second nature, and it's first class only. But back then, it was actually the first time some of us—including me—had ever been on a plane. So I can't tell you how much of an adventure it was for the team. Here we were, a bunch of ballplayers from the Midwest, flying to *Florida* for *Spring Training*. But despite all that, and the fact that a lot of us were pretty immature we behaved fairly well on the flight. With Coach Crockett hovering over us, you had to.

* * *

We touched down midmorning in Florida at West Palm Beach Airport. Through the Dodgertown people we'd hired a big old bus to get us to Vero Beach. So, after we retrieved all our bags and equipment from the luggage carousel, we helped load it into the storage compartments on the bus. Looking back, it was just like what I would experience down the road in the minors. But nobody was griping, despite the heat that hit us like a punch in the mouth once we exited the terminal. Because all around the building were *palm trees*, and girls on spring break from high school or college, walking around in short shorts and tank tops. Even Coach, who reminded us we were all here on a "business trip," stole a few glances at some of them, or maybe their moms. He was still single and in his early forties, after all.

The ride up Interstate 95 was a pretty straight shoot. We passed by Jupiter, Stuart, Fort Pierce, and Port St.

Lucie. From the highway they all looked the same. There were a lot of palm trees everywhere, however; and although we even saw some cattle pastures and citrus groves, the overall effect was much more pleasant than Missouri, for sure.

Finally, about an hour and a half up from West Palm, we entered the city limits of Vero Beach and turned off the highway.

I have since learned that like a lot of other communities along Florida's East Coast, Vero Beach is comprised of distinct areas that kind of got blended together. There is a main drag, US-1, that goes for a couple miles and has every department store and fast-food chain known to man. It could be Anywhere, USA. Then, if you go east towards the ocean, you have these ritzy gated communities with beautifully landscaped outer boundaries, and names like Casa du Mer, Sandy Shores and Vista Royale. You can then take a long bridge over the Indian River Inlet (Vero is in Indian River County) and end up at all the high-rise resorts, mansions, and restaurants that line the beach.

But where we were going was west of US-1. This was really where the original town sprang up in the early 1900s, and where the U.S. Navy decided to put an airbase during the Second World War.

The neighborhoods around Dodgertown were more blue-collar—not exactly run down, but more modest one-family, single-story bungalows. You could see where whole streets or developments, none of them with sidewalks, had been carved out of the jungle-like foliage that surrounded them. Most had barbecue grills in the yard, and a lot of people parked a car or two there as well, because there were few garages, only the occasional carport. And there were these canals everywhere, crisscrossing the various streets and avenues. Some were wide, with others only about six feet across or so. "Wonder what's in those canals, Bro," said Paco as our bus chugged past. I didn't want to think about it, because to this day I'm deathly afraid of snakes, and Florida's loaded with 'em. So, to put it simply, the Dodgertown area was a slice of "old Florida." It was in this area that for the first time I saw some Black folks.

Finally, we got onto Airline Drive, a stretch of road that led to our destination. As we approached the Dodgertown entrance, we could see small planes coming in for a landing at Vero Beach Airport, which was situated beyond the complex area and was the actual site of the runways for the airbase during the war. Then the entire bus started whooping and cheering as the ***Welcome to Historic Dodgertown*** sign came into view at the entrance to the team residence area. It was huge, with the lettering in Dodger blue over a white background, and it was surrounded by palm trees and multicolored tropical bushes that were obviously meticulously maintained. I have to say, it was pretty classy. And for just a second, I thought that everything might turn out okay.

* * *

Coach Crockett exited the bus outside the small registration building and went inside as we sat with the engine idling, looking out the windows at all the practice diamonds, which were separated by paved golf cart paths. Minutes later he emerged bearing a large brown envelope and hopped aboard. "All right, gentlemen," he said, addressing us from the top step, "I've got your room keys here. You got your rooming assignments before the trip, so let's get off the bus, take our equipment from the storage bins underneath, and I'll get you in your rooms to unpack. We'll meet right back out here in front of the registration building in a half hour. Then we'll be walking over to the conference center, which will be our dining hall, for lunch and orientation. So let's get after it."

Paco and I grabbed our bags and got our keys. The villas, as they were called, were situated along Sandy Koufax Lane. They were neat, one-story motel-like structures set side-by side, with small, tidy lawns out front and decorative tropical bushes along the walkways to the door. Basketball-sized lamppost globes shaped like baseballs, complete with red stitching, stood outside every unit. Once inside our villa, Paco and I threw our bags on the twin queen-sized beds and checked out the bathroom, which wasn't fancy, but functional. "This is where the players stayed during Spring Training," he said, "so I guess we're livin' large, Bro." We threw what few street clothes we'd brought, along with our bathing suits (we'd been told there was a pool we could use) in one dresser and stowed our uniforms and stuff in the other. Our bat bags were stood up in one corner. "I feel like a Major Leaguer already!" Paco said with a smile. "This sure beats my tiny room at home." He was from a big family, and their small house back in Kansas City was really cramped for space.

At 11:30 we walked over to the designated meeting area where the coaches were waiting. Spirits were high as the guys remarked on their big-league accommodations. Well, except for our resident prima donna, Trey Knight, who probably thought he deserved a single suite or something. Then we made our way down Jackie Robinson Avenue. Apparently, all the "streets" were named for famous old-time ballplayers, with blue and white signs and everything, which was cool. We reached the conference center, a modern facility with a Dodger blue awning, surrounded by palm trees. By this time everybody, including me, was getting hungry, and we wondered if the food would be better than what we were used to in our school's cafeteria.

We shouldn't have worried. A staff of workers in neat blue and white outfits had set out a buffet-style spread of sandwiches, salads, and fruit, with milk, real juices, and bottled water for us to enjoy. Though it was served cafeteria style, the quality of the food was anything but. Quickly, the guys loaded their trays, with some on the way to pigging out before Coach reminded them that we'd be practicing in an hour or so and he didn't want any of us weighed down. At that, a few of us off-loaded some unnecessary eats.

Our team was allotted three large circular tables in the room: infielders and outfielders at one; pitchers and catchers at another; and the coaches, their notes and schedules spread out before them, at a third. There was the usual chatter and light-hearted banter, and the eats were really good. Paco, who had a voracious appetite, polished off a couple sandwiches in no time and was about to go back for a third, when a middle-aged man wearing a Historic Dodgertown golf shirt and slacks entered. We could see him and Crockett share a hug and engage in a little small talk. Then, Coach asked for quiet so the man could address us.

"Hello, gentlemen," he began in a deep voice tinged with a Southern accent. "My name is Joe Burgos, and I'm the director of field activities here. On behalf of the entire staff, I'd like to welcome y'all to Florida, and Historic

Dodgertown. I'm so glad Coach Crockett and I were able to work out a way to get y'all down here for a week in the sun, where you'll get to play baseball all day long."

He paused while we applauded. "Let me tell you something, boys," he continued, "a week's stay at this place isn't cheap. Y'all should give it up for your coach to help swing this deal." Again, the guys burst into a hearty applause while Crockett waved us off. "Your team is gonna be enjoying Major League accommodations while you're here—from the way the fields and batting cages are maintained, to the cleanliness and comfort of your villas, to the food, which it seems you're enjoying already." More applause. "And that's fine. You'll get three healthy meals a day here, and our rule is simple: take all you want, but make sure you eat what you take. And if you feel the need to bring a couple pieces of fruit or some bottled water back to the villas, there is a mini fridge in each room for that. But don't overdo it."

I could see Coach Crockett shooting Paco a look and almost busted out laughing.

"Okay, now some basics. You guys will be operating on the main campus here—basically, everything on this side of the walkway bridge to Holman Stadium. You'll have maps in your room, but let me give you a visual." He pulled from the side of the room a large, mounted diagram of the complex and placed it on an easel. "Okay, so you came in the main entrance, and checked into the registration building. You've seen your villas, which extend in a line towards the back of the complex. A college men's soccer team will be working out on the multi-sport field across Roy Campanella Boulevard from this dining room. On the other side you'll find tennis and basketball courts and the pool.

"As far as your training areas, there are indoor batting cages a few steps away from this building, and Practice Fields 1, 2, and 3. There's also a specific pitching area with four mounds on the far side of this building. So, as you can see, you'll pretty much be restricted to this area except… should I tell them, Coach?"

Crockett nodded, a sly grin creasing his face.

"On Saturday, you *will* have to cross the footbridge, because we've arranged a doubleheader between you guys and Vero Beach High School, at Holman Stadium!"

There were some cheers and a lot of high-fives at the news.

Burgos grinned. "Oh, and one last thing. We have an athletic trainer on site who will be joining you for all your workouts, and she's top-notch. Her name is Amanda Lisnow, and she's a recent graduate of Florida State University who worked with their athletic teams throughout her college career. A word of advice, though, gentlemen: Don't mess with her. She takes her job seriously. So, y'all have a great time here, and I'll turn it over to Coach Crockett." He gave us a wave and exited.

"All right, guys," said Crockett. "Now here's where I read you the riot act. Most of what I'm going to tell you is in the KC South code of conduct, but it bears repeating." He cleared his throat.

"If there are any incidents involving drinking, drugs, fighting, or property damage in the villas, I'm putting your butt on the next plane home—on your parents' dime. You'll dress appropriately when on the campus outside the villas and treat all Historic Dodgertown staff with respect, right down to the person who rakes the infield. You'll place any trash outside your rooms each morning for pickup, which they'll do each day at 11:00 AM. If I get a report from housekeeping that your room is a pigsty, you're gonna run till your tongue's dragging on the ground—which shouldn't take long, because if you haven't noticed already, it's somewhat warm down here.

"Every morning we'll eat breakfast in this room at 7:30 AM, and practice will begin at 9 AM sharp. A practice schedule will be posted on this easel during breakfast for all to see. Figure on lunch at noon, and dinner at 6 PM. Lights out at ten. Don't make me and Coach Putney have to do bed checks. Anyway, guys, there's no place *to* go around here, in addition to the fact that you're all underage. Besides, the complex is bordered by an airport and some dense tropical undergrowth, and we wouldn't want a hungry gator making a midnight snack out of you."

This prompted some nervous laughter. Crockett, on a roll, continued:

"Just let me remind you that we are here on business. Our team has the opportunity to be special the season, and it all starts here. And as far as this place, it's incredible. There's so much history, you can feel it in the air. I invite you to check out all the framed photos on the walls when you're not stuffing your faces. The Brooklyn Dodgers were legendary, and the LA Dodgers are one of the most successful franchises in the Majors, one that every high school player should aspire to be a part of. While you're here, I want you to adopt the same mindset the thousands of players—including many Hall of Famers—had during Spring Training that made them successful. But overall, I just want you to drink it all in and have fun. This is the opportunity of a lifetime. Don't screw it up."

I could've sworn he gave me a sideways glance at those words, but maybe it was just my imagination.

"Let me finish with this. As Joe said, there will be a

local college soccer team practicing on the multipurpose field, but they're being bused in and returned to their campus each day because their athletic facility is being redone. And there's some kind of Little League camp being held all week on the practice diamonds behind Holman Stadium. Again, they'll be gone by late afternoon every day. So it's just us, gentlemen, and I can't wait to get started. Now, here's this afternoon's schedule: An hour from now, we'll meet on Practice Field 1 for stretching, calisthenics and sprints. Tee shirts, hats, shorts, and spikes. Then, I want all pitchers and catchers at the practice mounds next door with Coach Putney. I'll start in the batting cages with everybody else for some BP. Then, we'll move to Practice Field 2 for infield-outfield, and Field 3 for pitchers to work on pickoffs and covering first base. Any questions?"

Trey Knight raised his hand. "Uh, Coach, do we get some pool time?" he asked in his typically smarmy tone.

Crockett looked over at Trey and gave a thin smile, though we all sensed Coach couldn't stand him. However, he was the best pitcher we had, since I had flopped in that role. "Yes, Mr. Knight," he said patiently, "you will be free to use the pool each day between the end of our afternoon practice and dinner, if you so choose. However, since there's no lifeguard on site, we need at least one experienced swimmer present in any group that goes over there. And no horseplay around the pool."

"What about some swimming after dinner, Coach?" Knight pressed.

"Oh, that. Did I forget to mention we'll be doing an evening jog at 7:30? Thanks for reminding me, Trey."

"You're welcome, Coach," grumbled our ace as a few of the guys snickered.

* * *

Now, before I tell you about that first wonderful practice in Vero Beach, let me describe the key players on our team. You know all about Paco, who should have been all-district the year before as a junior, and our resident senior superstar and pain-in-the-butt, Trey. But there were some other guys worth mentioning.

First, we had a really solid infield. We called our third baseman, Donnie Pastorello, "Dirt Devil," because he'd suck up everything that came his way, even if he had to physically block it with his chest, or face. Plus, he had a gun for an arm. Then, there were the Bourke brothers, Bobby and Kevin, up the middle. These guys were twins, around 5'10" each, and I swear, you couldn't tell them apart. In fact, they were interchangeable in that they could both play second and short. Sometimes they just switched on their own during a game to amuse themselves, and tweak Crockett, and got away with it. And when one of them screwed up and Coach started chewing him out he'd say, "I didn't do it, Coach, it was my brother!" and so forth. But, man, they could sure turn the double play. And then we had our big first baseman, Mike Holland. We called him "Igor" because he kinda looked like Frankenstein, and even though he didn't have much range, he could hit the ball a mile. Best of all, from a pitcher's standpoint, we had three outfielders who could really go get it, especially our centerfielder, "Mercury" Mears, who regularly ran down balls in the gaps that would have rolled forever.

Overall, we had a solid mix of seniors and juniors as our starters, and although we were bringing a few sophomores down to Florida with us, they would mostly serve as fielding subs during the year. Crockett felt we could go a long way on our veteran leadership.

It was our pitching that was suspect—beginning with me, of course. Because after the great Trey, who was a right-hander like me, there were only two guys, both junior lefties who had good control but couldn't bring it like Trey and me. Oh, by the way, we had two backups for Paco: Frank Lammers, who wasn't as adept as Paco at calling a game or digging balls out of the dirt; and a sophomore, Babe MacAuley, who got the nickname 'cause he couldn't hit a lick. So, why had he made the team, you ask? Because we needed an emergency catcher, for one thing; and because he served as Trey's personal valet. Babe happily agreed to room with Knight on this trip when nobody else wanted to. Man, I think he probably made the guy's bed every morning. Which was why everybody mercilessly ragged on him. But Babe didn't care. It got him to Vero Beach, right?

* * *

After lunch we waddled back to the villas, noting that it had gotten considerably warmer while we were eating. "Shouldn't have had that extra piece of pie," mumbled Paco with a burp as he pulled on his protective cup.

"Hey, when we go to the pitching mounds, try to catch me," I said nervously. "I know Trey will want to have you, but I'd feel more comfortable with you today."

"Can't imagine why," he said sarcastically. "I'll try, Bro, but Putney has final say on who catches who."

We got our stuff together and strolled over to Practice Field 3, where everyone was milling about. At exactly 1:30 PM, Coach had us all take a long lap around the field. Then, as was our normal routine, we did some soft-tossing and then got into a big circle, with the coaches in the middle. From there, Crockett led us through a good half hour of stretches and light calisthenics. I swear, we stretched better than most MLB clubs, and the proof was that we hardly ever had any muscle pulls. Then we lined up for some three-quarter speed form-running sprints, lifting our knees high and stuff like that. The sun was shining brightly, and there was a slight breeze that made the palm trees lining the paved paths sway. It was like a picture postcard, man.

Then, suddenly, Coach blew his whistle, and we broke up and jogged to our designated areas. You never walked on Crockett's practice field. When he said, "On the hop, gentlemen," he meant it.

When our group reached the row of practice mounds, Coach Putney paired us off; as I expected, Trey got Paco. But then our lefties, Timmy Galvin and Rick Sages, got put with Frankie Lammers, leaving me with Babe, who was only a marginally better defensive catcher than hitter. "Hope you brought your protective equipment, son," cracked Trey to the sophomore, which ticked me off.

"I'm ready," he answered bravely as he strapped on his shin guards. "C'mon, Darnell." Babe motioned me over to the farthest mound and I followed, still stewing. I mean, based on what I'd become, I didn't merit any more than our third stringer; but when you're seventeen years old it's hard to think that maturely.

"Start off three-quarter speed, fellas," said Putney, who stood behind the six-foot chain-link backstop that ran the length of the multi-mound area. "Get loose, and then we'll just go with fastballs today. We've got all week, remember."

And so, that's what we did—except Trey, of course, who put a little extra on his early throws, and sneaked in a slider, his specialty pitch, which ticked off Paco. "Yo, Bro, the man said three-quarters fastballs," he snarled at our ace.

"Oops, sorry," said Trey. "Can't help myself."

"Yeah, right."

When I signaled to Putney that I was all warmed up, he said, "Okay, Darnell. Now remember, free and easy. Let's stay with the no-windup approach, okay?"

"Sure, Coach."

So Babe squatted, gave his glove a pound, and held it out waist-high.

I promptly fired my first pitch over his head.

Luckily, we'd all been provided with a bucket of balls, so Babe didn't have to keep going to the backstop when I skipped one or sailed it—which was nearly every pitch. The other guys, who were trying to concentrate on their own workouts, couldn't help but cast sideways glances at me. And I know I heard Knight snicker a time or two.

Of course, I became Coach Putney's project for the day, and he ended up standing behind my mound, whispering words of encouragement and suggesting a slight adjustment here, there, and everywhere. By the time the session was over, I couldn't hit water if I fell out of a boat. You don't know how relieved I was when we heard Crockett's whistle to move to Field 3 for fielding drills and pickoffs. I couldn't help noticing, though, that he and Putney exchanged a few words when they passed each other during the transition, ending with our pitching coach shaking his head. I felt awful.

"Yo, Bro, what the hell?" whispered Paco as he removed his shin guards. "You trying to kill MacAuley, or what? He's going to have welts on top of his welts."

"Thanks," I said.

Fortunately, the drills went better. Truth be told, I was the most athletic of all the pitchers, by far. I actually enjoyed fielding bunts and covering first base. And, for a righty, I had a fairly good pickoff move. It was the actual pitching stuff I couldn't do.

It was during these drills that our athletic trainer Amanda showed up. She was built like a square of granite, with Dodger blue cargo shorts and a white golf shirt. Her hair was cut short, and she had on a blue visor and Oakley shades. Around her waist was a belt with all kinds of roles of tape, scissors, and whatnot. That guy Burgos was right—the lady was all business. Trey was about to say something wise when Paco whispered, "Zip it, *amigo*, she'd break you in half." For once, the idiot listened.

Our group ended the day in the batting cages, but I just couldn't get comfortable. I kept recalling my horrendous mound session, while at the same time realizing that most—if not all—our outfielders this year were as good or better than me. I had one place on this team, and I wasn't even close to being able to handle it. So my mind began working on an exit strategy. By the time BP was over, I started to execute my brilliant plan.

"Excuse me, Miss?" I said to Amanda, who was watching from behind the cage as the JUGS mechanical pitching gun fired fastballs at Frankie Lammers.

"Call me Amanda," she said without smiling. "What's up?"

"I've, uh, got a little shoulder tightness," I said.

So, she walked me over to the metal bleachers near Field 2, had me sit down, and started moving my arm this way and that, manipulating it here and there, and throwing in an occasional "Does this hurt?" When I started stammering my responses she whispered, "Hey, I saw you airmailing those pitches before. You sure your shoulder's tight?"

Man, was I that transparent? All I could do was hang my head. But then, God bless her, Amanda the trainer saved me. "Coach," she called, waving Crockett over, "your pitcher's got a little first-day shoulder stiffness. Probably airing it out a little too early. I say we slap an ice pack on it and let him rest it till tomorrow—but he's done for the day, I think."

"Sure thing," said Crockett before jogging back to the infield-outfield drills.

When he was gone, she looked into my eyes. "All right, kid, I got you a reprieve till tomorrow," she said, "so you'd better figure this all out by breakfast."

"Okay, thanks," I gratefully replied.

"Tell you what, though," she said. "Not only is there nothing wrong with your arm, you've got enough velocity to pitch in college." I was about to thank her when she added, "Of course, you got no clue where the ball is going, which could be an issue."

* * *

I pretty much moped around the villa after practice, while most of the other guys went for a dip in the pool. I realized that the fake injury thing wasn't gonna fly and racked my brain for a dignified way out. I absolutely dreaded going to practice the next morning. Probably on purpose, Paco came back a little early from the pool, a towel slung over his muscular shoulder. "Man, there's nothin' like wearin' flip-flops in April," he said, lying back on his bed. "And dinner's in an hour. We're livin' large, Bro."

"You know it," I said.

"Guys were talking at the pool," he said casually.

"About what?"

"You."

"Oh yeah?"

"Don't try and play it off, Bro," he said. "They're startin' with the 'Head Case Hayward' stuff again. You gotta get your act together, pronto."

"Don't you think I'm trying?" I said.

"I know you are," he said quietly. "But *they* don't know that. You're not exactly easy to get to know. And Trey being a wiseass isn't helping."

"He's ragging on me?"

"What do *you* think?"

I took a deep breath. "What if I tell Crockett I want to go home?"

"*What*? After one day? Naw, man, that's not cool. At least stay overnight. Then, if you feel the same way tomorrow, you tell him. I just don't want you to do something you'll regret later. You gotta be sure on this, Bro."

"And why's that?"

He turned to me, and he had the most serious face I'd ever seen on him. "Because you've got a gift, Darnell. The most I'll ever be—maybe—is a junior college player. But you? With that arm, you could go a long way, maybe even to the Majors."

"You think?"

He smiled. "I *know*. So, let's just go have a good meal and do our dopey team run and get a good night's sleep. And I guarantee you, you'll feel better tomorrow."

"You really believe that?"

"Your catcher knows best, Bro."

Paco was, and is, the best friend I ever had.

* * *

Dinner that night was great—we had our choice of roast turkey or prime rib—but my food seemed tasteless. Then, about halfway through the meal, Crockett got up and came over to my table, and he tapped me on the shoulder. "Got a minute?" he asked.

"Sure, Coach," I said, and he walked me outside as everyone watched. It was a beautiful spring late afternoon; the breeze had picked up a bit, cooling the complex.

"Isn't this place great?" he said, starting things off. "Hard to believe it began as a military training base."

"Yeah, it's pretty cool," I said, my stomach in knots.

"How's the shoulder?" he asked.

"What?"

"Your shoulder, Darnell. Did it loosen up?"

"Oh, oh yeah," I said. "I think the ice really helped. That Amanda really knows what she's doing."

"Good, good," he said. "So, you think you'll be ready to get after it again tomorrow?"

I couldn't tell him the truth. "Sure," I said.

He looked me square in the eye. "Listen," he said, "no matter what Trey thinks, a lot of what we'll be this year depends on you. I know you're feeling the pressure, but I think you've got to give it a chance."

I came so close to quitting right then, telling him that I appreciated the concern but that it was hopeless… but I chickened out. "Thanks, Coach," I said.

"C'mon, let's go get some dessert before Paco eats it all," he said, and we went back inside.

* * *

After the team jog, which was actually somewhat pleasant, we returned to the villas as it was getting dark. Once inside our room, Paco asked me what Crockett and I had talked about. "He thinks you eat too much," I joked.

"Yeah, right. Ain't nobody blocks the plate like me, Bro. Come on, spill it. What'd you *really* talk about?"

"He asked me how my shoulder was, is all," I said.

"And you told him what?"

"I told him it was feeling much better."

"Almost like it never happened, right?" he said with a raised eyebrow.

I fired a pillow at him—a perfect strike.

Chapter Four
The First Night

I've always been a light sleeper. It takes me a long time to drift off, and even the slightest noise will wake me up. And if I have stuff on my mind, forget it. These days I use melatonin, but I had no knowledge of the stuff that first night in Vero Beach. Paco, on the other hand, had no trouble falling asleep after what would become his customary one hour of video games on his phone. Frankly, our whole team had every right to be exhausted that first night. We'd flown in from Kansas City, had a full practice, dinner, and a leisurely twilight jog with the coaches before going back to the villas. I would've been surprised if anyone in the complex was awake after 10 PM. Except me, of course.

It's not like I didn't try. After a long, hot shower, I'd come out of the bathroom to find my catcher dead asleep and snoring. So I got in my bed and tried my best to nod off. But the events of this day, and what I was going to do during the next one, had me tossing and turning.

Finally, way past eleven, I gave up and pulled on a tee shirt, shorts and sneakers, figuring that a late-night stroll around the complex would clear my mind and give me the chance to formulate and plan my exit from the team, as well as what I was going to say to my parents when Crockett called them to announce that I was coming home—at their expense—and that they'd have to pick up their failure of a son at the airport.

So I slipped out of the villa, quietly pulling the door closed behind me, and breathed in the humid Florida air. I remember there was a faint, swampy smell of vegetation, probably from the creek running underneath the footbridge that separated the practice part of Dodgertown from Holman Stadium. It had six-foot high banks on each side that were choked with lush tropical greenery, all kinds of twisting vines and palm-type bushes and trees that could be seen from the outfield fences of the practice fields as we'd jogged by earlier. And I had no doubt that there were lots of creepy- crawly things in the foot and a half of water that meandered through that vegetation.

But the moon was full and bright, and the muted glow from those many baseball lampposts outside the villas—as well as a few traditional pole lights that dotted the various paths—gave the grounds a pleasant, low-key atmosphere. And you could hear *everything*, man. Bullfrogs, night birds, cicadas. There was a breeze, but not much.

I started walking, past the practice mounds where I'd made a fool of myself today, then the batting cages and diamonds, their dirt infields outlined against the dark grass. I was trying to figure out what I was gonna do, and when, so none of the guys would witness my act of quitting. Then I decided that before I left, I might as well stroll over to Holman Stadium and get a look at it, since I'd never actually get a chance to play there. Of course, I'd have to cross that footbridge and whatever was slithering around underneath it to get there. But hey, it only looked to be about fifty feet long and it dozen feet wide; so if I stayed in the middle, I figured nothing could jump up and bite me.

That's when I saw the guy. On the footbridge. Alone.

He was about midway across, leaning on the railing, looking off into the jungle. Now, it was weird enough that he was out there at all in the middle of the night, but there was also his clothes. He was wearing what I guessed was a light-colored golf shirt, and a pair of khaki or white slacks, sharply creased, with lace-up tan shoes. That, in itself, was fairly normal. But he wore his pants high up on his hips, to the point where if the guys on my team saw him, they'd start making jokes.

So now I had to decide if I was gonna turn tail and go back to the villas or pass this dude on the bridge. At first, his size—I estimated his height at about six feet, with an athletic build—had me a little intimidated. But then, he turned, and the moonlight caught his face, and I could see his neatly trimmed hair was gray on the sides. In fact, he was pretty handsome for a white guy, square-jawed, with a cleft chin. Very distinguished looking, you know? So I figured he was no threat, and kept going forward.

You know how sometimes there are moments in your life that just stay with you? Well, one of mine came when the guy with his pants pulled up too high turned to me and said, "Well, Willie, what brings you out here at this time of night?"

I stopped cold. Who was this dude, and why was he calling me Willie? "Excuse me?" I said.

"You're Willie… Willie Jackson. One of the minor leaguers in camp this year," he said in a soothing voice.

"My name's Ed," he said, extending his hand. Hesitantly, I took it. The grip was firm.

And ice cold.

I had the urge to jerk my hand back but didn't. The man's eyes were blue and friendly. Something told me I shouldn't fear him. But why was he calling me by my grandfather's name? I mean, I'd been told I resembled him in his younger days, but still. My head was spinning. "Hi… Ed," I managed.

"So, why are you out here so late?" he asked again.

"Couldn't sleep."

"How come?"

"Worrying, I guess."

"About what?"

"Uh, making the team."

"Yeah," he said, "I understand. But from what I hear, you're pretty good. You came from the Monarchs, right?"

Now there was no doubt. This guy knew my grandfather, and thought I was him. But how could that be possible if he looked to be in his thirties? And why was he talking to me like it was back in the day? I had no clue what to do. I mean, what if this guy was a psycho? What if he had a knife or something? He could kill me and toss me off the bridge and nobody would hear anything… and they wouldn't find me till the next morning—unless I got eaten by some gator, that is. Fighting back my panic, I decided to play along.

"Yeah, that's me," I said. "I pitched for the Monarchs."

"That's a top-notch Negro team," he said, oblivious to the fact that nobody says 'Negro' anymore. "So what's your problem with making the ballclub?"

"You mean the Dodgers?" I said.

"Well, sure."

"It's pretty simple," I said with a shrug. "I forgot how to throw strikes."

He chuckled. "That could be a problem," he said. "My guess is that you're putting so much pressure on yourself that it's blocking you physically from doing things that you'd ordinarily do naturally." He leaned back against the railing.

"There's also what you're probably hearing from outside sources—your teammates and coaches. They see a guy who has all the talent, but who can't live up to their expectations. So, I'm assuming they're either overloading you with advice or criticizing you, and that never helps.

"Baseball is a humbling game, Willie. There are so many times that your confidence will be shaken so badly you'll want to quit it forever. And that's even if you become really good at it. A hitting slump or the inability to throw strikes can just gnaw at you. Believe me, I know. But you've just got to be able to shake it off and trust in your ability."

Ed's voice was calm and measured, but his eyes were intense. It was clear he had experienced some tough times in his own life. Then he paused, like he was measuring me. "You seem like a nice kid, Willie," he said. "Why don't we do this: Come back tomorrow night and we'll meet up. Bring your glove and spikes. I'll bet we can get all this figured out."

"You think so?"

"Couldn't hurt. It's worth a try, anyway. Are you game?"

"Sure," I said. "But why would you want to help me?"

"Because that's what we do here," he answered with a sweep of his arm.

"At Dodgertown?"

"Well, of course."

"Oh, okay then," I said.

"See you tomorrow," he said, then turned away and began walking towards Holman Stadium.

I started back across the bridge, but after a couple steps I thought of a question to ask him and turned back.

Ed was gone.

Chapter Five
Day Two

I awakened from a restless sleep to see my catcher hovering over the bed, already dressed. "*Que pasa*, Sleeping Beauty! It's a bee-utiful Tuesday morning in Florida! And if you don't get your sorry butt out of bed you're gonna miss breakfast."

My mind still reeling from the night before, I pulled on some clothes and was ready in a flash. God forbid I made Paco late for a meal. "How'd you sleep, Bro?" he asked as we exited the villa, stepping into another day of brilliant sunshine.

"Not too bad," I answered. I had decided not to let him, or anyone else, in on my midnight stroll and the very weird encounter with high-pockets Ed. They all thought I was a head case already.

"So how's the shoulder?" he asked. "You ready to throw?"

"Don't know exactly," I said, hedging. "Let me see what Coach says."

"Uh-huh." I could tell Paco wasn't buying the whole shoulder tightness thing, but he wouldn't come out and say it. And for that, I was grateful.

Gradually the entire team straggled in, with Trey (and his personal assistant Babe) making a grand entrance just before the clock hit half past seven. As we dined on a healthy breakfast of fresh fruit, cereals and granola, Crockett and Putney laid out the practice schedule for the day. Basically, it was just an expanded version of the previous day's activities, broken up into two sessions with lunch in between.

"Make sure you keep hydrating all the time," Crockett warned. "It's sneaky hot out there, and none of us are acclimated to it right now." One thing about Coach: even though he was old-school like I said, he really believed in getting your fluids—which, of course, kept you on the field. I swear, if one of us ever dropped from heat exhaustion, he'd be standing over the guy and yelling that he'd forgotten to hydrate. Today we'd be practicing in our three-quarter sleeve undershirts and game pants, and I wondered, as I glanced up at one of those ancient Brooklyn Dodgers framed photos that dotted the walls, how those guys survived in the old woolen flannel uniforms they wore.

I was just finishing my Cheerios with sliced bananas when Putney materialized at my side. "Why don't we ease off a bit today," he said. "I think yesterday you put your foot on the gas too soon. We've got to build up your strength gradually, Darnell."

I nodded, and Trey said, "Yes, we do, Darnell" with a smirk.

"Zip it, Trey," snapped Paco.

"Yessir, Coach Gonzalez," he replied with a smart salute. Paco just slitted his eyes. Boy, he hated Knight.

* * *

I wish I could tell you that my second day of Spring Training went well, but it was just as bad as the first. No, worse. Because by the end of the morning session I was questioning my decision to hold off on quitting. That was because I nearly killed my pitching coach.

No joke.

We were done with stretching and calisthenics and soft-tossing and found ourselves back on the practice mounds. Again, I had Babe MacAuley assigned to me. This time he'd strapped on every piece of protective equipment he could find; and at first I was okay, 'cause I was throwing real slow and deliberate. So what happened? Well, in an effort to somehow pump me up psychologically, Coach Putney put on a batting helmet, grabbed a bat, and stood in to face me. "I'm not going to swing or anything, Darnell," he assured. "Just take it up a notch and stick with the fastball."

I nodded, and immediately broke out in a cold sweat. To make things worse, my good buddy Trey stopped throwing, faking like he was rubbing up a ball, and looked over. "C'mon, Darnell," said Babe, pounding his mitt and giving me a target. "Right here!"

If only.

So I rocked back in my no-windup motion, kicked, and dealt a fastball that caught Putney right above the earhole. As he crumpled to the ground, the ball shot like twenty feet in the air.

"Dang," said Trey, as everyone else sprinted to our stricken coach.

And me? I just stood there frozen and tried not to throw up. I thought Putney was dead.

I guess the thing that snapped me back to reality was when Amanda crossed my line of vision in her dash to aid my victim. After she'd knelt next to Putney for a few seconds, I was relieved to see him stir, then sit up. It was only then that I could get my feet to move as I shuffled towards him. "Hoo boy," I heard him say. "That was close."

"I-I'm sorry, Coach," I said, trying my hardest not to start crying.

"No big deal, Darnell," he replied with a feeble wave. "I was probably leaning in too far, and I keep forgetting I have the reflexes of a forty-year-old." He asked the guys clustered around him to help him up.

"You okay, Coach?" said Amanda, closely monitoring his movements, probably for signs of a concussion, as he rose to his feet.

"Oh, sure," he said, managing a grin. "It didn't catch me flush."

"Could've fooled me," said Trey, fingering the helmet he'd picked up off the ground. "I think there's a pretty big crack in the side there."

Then I threw up.

* * *

I moped my way through lunch, and nobody at my table said much. To say it was awkward is an understatement. Because word had got around pretty quick that I'd almost brained our coach. Even when Putney came over and whispered in my ear not to worry about it, I was still mortified. Finally, on the way out of the conference center, Crockett ran me down. "You okay?" he asked, studying my face.

"Yeah," I lied.

"Listen," he said, "what happened this morning, it's a part of the game. Better now than during the season. Coach Putney should know better than to jump in the batter's box anyway."

"He was trying to build me up," I said.

"I get that, Darnell. But still." He stopped me and looked me in the eye. "You want to go home, son?"

There it was. My chance to escape, served up on a silver platter. I thought of the sound the ball made cracking off my coach's helmet... the sight of him sagging to the ground... Trey's wiseass remark. But then, I saw that guy Ed's face and remembered my promise to be there tonight. Talk about conflicted. "I'm not sure, Coach," I said.

He squinted up into the sun. "Tell you what," he said, his hands crossing his chest and tucked under his armpits like when he was arguing with an umpire, "you go with the outfielders for the afternoon practice, and tomorrow morning, you tell me what you want to do. Whatever you decide, I'll respect your decision. But I'd rather not lose you from the team. You good with that?"

"Yessir," I said.

"Fine. We'll see you at the batting cage in twenty minutes."

And that was that.

So I spent the afternoon taking BP, shagging fly balls, and practicing cutoff throws with the other outfielders, barely able to hide my shame at the demotion. I'll say this, though: when I connected solidly with the baseball during BP it felt great. Because all the while I was pretending it was Trey's head.

That evening, I didn't know whether to sit at the pitcher's table or with the fielders. But Paco, God bless him, anticipated my dilemma, and pulled out a chair for me next to his when I slinked into the conference center. And even though my stomach had still been queasy for a while after I'd puked—I'd hardly touched my lunchtime sandwich—I managed to get down the pasta and meatballs that were served up. Just like at lunch, the guys tried to maintain the usual smart-alecky chatter you found at our gatherings, but it was strained, like they were almost forcing it. I ate quickly and left. And as we soldiered through our evening jog later on, I actually found myself awaiting, with a mixture of excitement and fear, my next midnight walk in Dodgertown.

Chapter Six
The Second Night

Once I was sure Paco was sound asleep, I pulled on a baseball undershirt, sweatpants and socks and crept out of our villa, carrying my spikes, glove, and a bag of balls. Again the moon shone brightly, and there was the hint of a breeze coming in from the ocean some ten miles away. Truth be told, I was scared, and put off walking towards the footbridge for as long as I could. But finally I thought, "Screw it. High-pockets Ed probably won't be there anyway."

As I passed the chain-link outfield fence of Practice Field 1 and approached the footbridge, I saw I was not only wrong, but that there were *two* guys there. "Oh, great," I muttered to myself.

"Hey, Willie," said Ed, this time attired in what looked like a bowling shirt, with those hiked-up trousers. "Glad to see you could make it." He extended his hand for a shake, and again his skin had that strange clammy feel.

"Good to see you too, Ed," I replied as the other man looked on with curiosity.

Ed then pointed to the guy, who was dressed in pretty much the same style; but he was a few inches shorter, with longish, light brown hair, combed straight back with a side part. "This is my friend Harold," he said. "He knows a lot about baseball, maybe even more than me. I told him about the problems you're having, and he asked if he could tag along tonight. You don't mind, do you?"

"No, not at all," I said, becoming more comfortable with the whole 'Willie' thing. "Glad to meet you, Harold," I said, extending my hand.

Jeez, his skin was even colder than Ed's. I tried not to cringe. "Nice to meet you too, Willie," said Harold, breaking into a wide grin that eased my tension a bit. He had a bit of a Southern drawl, and an easy-going manner that made me trust him immediately. "My buddy here's been filling me in on your difficulties. Maybe I can help if you'd want me to."

"That would be fine," I said.

"Well, good then," said Harold. "I see you brought your spikes and glove. Great. Let's go over to the ball field and see what you've got."

"Sure thing," I said. I started to walk towards Holman Stadium, which stood out against the moonlit sky.

"No, not there, Willie," said Ed. "Let's go back to one of the practice diamonds."

I was confused. "But, it's dark—"

"That won't be a problem," said Harold.

So, I shrugged and retreated towards the practice fields, with Ed and Harold behind me. "Uh, which field, guys?" I said.

"Let's go to that wall over yonder," said Harold. "Just to get the lay of the land, okay?"

"Sure," I said.

Off towards the side of Practice Field 3 there was a

ten-foot high by six-foot wide concrete wall that was painted white, with a red box where the strike zone was. Facing the wall sixty feet, six inches away was a solitary pitching mound. Harold motioned me to take the mound.

"You want me to throw?" I said, immediately feeling stupid.

"That's the idea, Willie," said Ed. "We just want to check out your motion."

"Okay," I said.

They stood behind the mound as I climbed on top, dropped the bag of balls next to the pitching rubber, and loosened my arm up. I can't tell you how nervous I was. I mean who *were* these guys, and why was I letting myself be scrutinized by them? But then again, it didn't seem like I had much of a choice in the matter.

"Nice and easy, Willie," said Harold. "Show us your fastball." So, I rocked back and let it go… over the wall. I wanted to die.

"A little high," said Harold with a chuckle. "Calm down, Willie. We're all on the same team here. I can see that you throw hard. Just stop trying to make a hole in the concrete."

So I kept throwing. Gradually I found the range, so that I was at least *hitting* the wall. The *thwock* of horsehide striking concrete echoed throughout the empty complex. I started calming down a little. But there was something else going on, something strange. See, when I first got on the mound, I could barely make out the outline of the wall in the moonlight. But the more I threw, the brighter it got, like there was a floodlight right over our little area. It was weird, man. But the two guys I was with didn't even seem to notice.

As I threw I could hear Ed and Harold whispering

behind me. It sounded mostly serious, with an occasional giggle thrown in. But they were just out of earshot, so I could only imagine their critiques. Of course, this made it even more stressful for me, and I rarely hit the red box.

Finally, after I'd emptied the bag, Harold said, "That's enough, Willie. We've seen what we came to see."

"What?" I snapped. "That I can't hit water if I fell out of a boat?"

Harold chuckled. "No, no, nothing that dramatic. You throw hard enough, but you are definitely all screwed up. And what's wrong here is kinda outside our area of expertise."

I said, "Well, thanks anyway—"

"But we know someone else who can help you," Ed cut in.

"Oh, really?" I said, somewhat sarcastically. "And who would *that* be?"

"Well," drawled Harold, sensing my annoyance, "if you're willin' to come back one more time, you can meet him. But it's your decision."

I took a deep breath. This would lock me in for another day down here, and effectively end any chance of me going home. "You really think this guy can help me?" I said, a little more humbly.

"Oh yeah," said Harold. "He's top-notch on pitching techniques and all that."

"But it's up to you, Willie," said Ed in that smooth voice of his.

"And you really think there's a chance I can improve?"

"I've seen sicker cows get well," said Harold with a smile. "Listen, Willie, players come and go. Now while I agree that luck can have a lot to do with success, there's no substitute for hard work and the willingness to listen to those who really want to help you. I can tell you without a doubt that support from people, especially the guys on the team, can make all the difference. But again, it all comes down to how bad you want to succeed. So, are you in or not?"

"I'm in, guys," I said. "Same time tomorrow night at the bridge?"

"Sure thing," said Ed. "We'll be waiting for you. So why don't you gather up those balls and get yourself a good night sleep."

"Okay. And… thanks, guys," I said.

"Happy to help," said Harold. 'Night, Willie." With that, the pair turned and walked back into the darkness on the way to the bridge. The light over the pitching wall faded out.

I bagged the baseballs and went back to the villas, still confused but oddly encouraged.

<h1 style="text-align:center">Chapter Seven</h1>
Day Three

The next morning I awoke with at least a semblance of hope, I and didn't hesitate to take my place at the pitchers and catchers table in the conference center. Predictably, Crockett sought me out during the meal to find out how I was doing. He motioned me over to the side of the room, away from the guys. "So, what are you thinking today, Darnell?" he asked, sipping from a go-cup of coffee.

"I'm staying, Coach," I said. "For better or worse."

"Good man," he replied. "And it's gonna get better, you watch."

"I hope so," I said. "There's just one thing, though."

"And what's that?"

"I want to go with the pitchers. I'm not ready to give up on that."

"I was hoping you'd say that," he said. "We really need you in the rotation. I just don't want to see you get down on yourself like yesterday. You know, I really believe that a positive outlook is…"

But I was tuning him out at this point, because I was focused on an old black-and-white framed picture on the wall over Coach's shoulder. It showed two of the old Brooklyn Dodgers on the top step of the dugout at their home ballpark, Ebbets Field. Both of them were holding bats, which casually rested on their shoulder. The caption underneath the photos read ***Duke Snider and Pee Wee Reese***. But I knew them as Ed and Harold.

* * *

I walked back to the villas in a fog. We only had a little while to digest our food and grab our stuff for the morning practice, but I immediately got on my phone and Googled those guys. What I found made me lightheaded.

Edwin "Duke" Snider was the Dodgers' centerfielder during their golden era of the 1940s and '50s. He was also an amazing power hitter from the left side and a graceful fielder. Snider had been born in California and was a multi-sport athlete in high school. Although he was pursued by the Cincinnati Reds and St. Louis Cardinals, he signed with the Dodgers. After serving in the U.S. Navy during World War II, he reported to the Dodgers' Spring Training camp—at that time in Bear Mountain, New York—where he worked out with Brooklyn's minor leaguers. Everyone could see the guy had talent, but he had no clue of the strike zone, kind of the same problem I was having. Once he got that down, though, he made the big club and went on to become one of its most iconic stars, "The Duke of Flatbush." By the time he was done, he'd collected more than 2,000 hits and 400 homers in the Majors and was elected to the Baseball Hall of Fame in 1980.

His buddy, Harold "Pee Wee" Reese, from Louisville, Kentucky, was the shortstop and captain of the Dodgers from the 1940s through their move to Los Angeles in '58. In his fifteen seasons with the club, the Dodgers won seven National League pennants. So, although his stats wouldn't blow you away compared to today's players, the guy's all-around talent and leadership made him a Hall of Famer, too. And just as important, I learned that he'd helped set the example with his teammates by openly accepting Jackie Robinson when he joined the team in 1947. For a guy from the South to do this, especially back in the day, it was pretty impressive. And even though I'd only met him once, I got that same supportive vibe from him, even though he was calling me by my grandfather's name.

So, the fact that I'd met these two all-time great Dodgers, and that they actually wanted to help me, was pretty unbelievable. The other thing that made it pretty unbelievable was that they were both dead.

* * *

"So, you're stickin' it out, Bro?" asked Paco as we strolled over to Practice Field 2 for the morning stretch.

"Looks like it," I said.

"Good. I'm not used to sleeping alone." He gave me a playful punch in the shoulder, and I snapped a jab at him, too. "So what changed your mind?"

"I don't know, man," I said, keeping my midnight rendezvous with dead people to myself. "Just a feeling. Besides, I'd be an idiot to give up this beautiful sunshine for the rain and sleet they're getting back home."

"You got that right. You workin' out with the pitchers today?"

"Yup."

"Solid. Just try not to kill anybody, okay?" he cracked.

"I'll do my best."

So, we circled up for stretching and cals, and for the first time, I really tried to relax and take it in: the fragrance of the freshly cut grass, the riffling of the palm fronds overhead… the *chuk-chuk-chuk* of sprinklers on an adjacent field. It was a glorious day to be out there playing baseball, in a place that I was starting to believe was, like PawPaw said, a little bit magical.

Of course, there was always Trey to screw things up. "You're back with us?" he teased as we broke into our groups for drills. "I thought you were converting to the outfield."

"Nope," I said. "I was afraid you'd miss me."

Paco chuckled.

"Hey, I got no problem with that," Knight said innocently. "As long as you pull your weight. I can't go out there and pitch every day, you know. Gotta take care of this arm. It's gonna make me a lot of money someday."

"Uh-huh," I said.

"He's gonna be fine," snapped Paco. "Just give it a little time."

"What are you, his agent or something?" Trey shot back.

"No. Just his catcher, Bro." The murderous look on his face convinced Trey to chill out.

Luckily, Coach Putney let Paco catch me on this morning, and though I was all over the place again, he managed to minimize the damage by his defensive acrobatics. Smartly, Putney refrained from stepping in against me again. But I have to admit, my mind was somewhere else that morning, because I was having a hard time wrapping my head around the implications of what had happened the previous two nights.

Here's the problem: I'm not a religious guy in

general, but back in high school, I was even more out of touch with things of that nature. My parents had been raised Baptist, but they had pretty much gotten away from attending Sunday services and stuff like that. I believed in God and all, but it's not like I was fervent about it. So, if you asked me back then if I believed in an afterlife, I would've just shrugged my shoulders.

So then, how could I explain talking to two guys who were no longer of this world? Guys who seemed pretty solid, not vapory ghosts? Who had a grip—albeit a cold one—when they shook my hand?

And there was something else. It's not like they were old, decrepit men; they seemed to be fairly young guys, like in the picture that hung on the wall in the conference center. And then I figured, if they knew my grandfather, they must be living in this alternate universe where it's the year he went to Spring Training in Vero Beach. I decided to give my folks a call during my lunch break to pin down the year and give some kind of clarity to what was happening to me. That is, if I wasn't just having a complete nervous breakdown and imagining the whole deal. And believe me, I was having thoughts about that, too.

* * *

So, before heading over to the conference center for lunch, I waited till Paco had left and placed a call to Kansas City. Naturally, my mom was nervous that something was wrong, but after I assured her that I was doing great, I asked her to find out from my grandfather what year he'd gone to camp with the Brooklyn Dodgers. She came back a few minutes later and said, "Honey, he's pretty sure it was 1953, though you can't be positive about his memory sometimes. He wondered why you wanted to know."

"Just curious," I said nonchalantly. "It's kind of strange being here in the same place he trained and all."

She seemed satisfied with that response. "Are you enjoying yourself?" she asked.

"Oh yeah. It's been fine," I said. "The weather's great, and the accommodations and food are first-class."

"How's your training going?"

"Coming along, Mom," I said. "Gotta build up my arm strength and all that, but everything's going fine," I lied.

"That's good to hear," she said, "because I sensed you weren't too enthusiastic about going down there in the first place."

"Why would you think that?"

"Because no one knows you better than your mama," she replied tartly. "And don't you forget it."

"I won't. Give my best to Dad and PawPaw." I clicked off and went to eat.

* * *

With my mind working overtime with this news about my grandfather, I entered the conference center to see Coach Crockett in conversation with Joe Burgos, probably about their baseball careers back in the day or something. So, after I loaded my tray and staked out a place at the pitchers and catchers table next to Paco, I went over to have a word with Mr. Burgos.

"So, you'd like some information on Dodgertown?" he asked with a broad smile. "That's good to hear,

Darnell. Today's players, even in the pros, don't care much about the past."

"Well," I said, nodding towards Crockett, "Coach has done his best to try to get us into it, but I found out something just now that's got me really interested."

"What's that?"

"My grandfather, Willie Jackson, was a pitcher in the Negro Leagues with the Kansas City Monarchs," I said. "The Dodgers actually had him come to camp here, I think in 1953. But that was his only year. So, I'm kind of interested in that season, and whether I can find out what happened to him. Why he didn't make it, you know."

"Gee, I didn't know that about your granddad," said Crockett. "Is that something you can help him with, Joe?"

Burgos frowned. "Listen, I know a lot about the history of this place, but I'm not an expert," he confessed. "However, I do know of someone who might be able to help. His name is Charlie Sutton, and he was here working for the Dodgers when they first came to Vero Beach and stayed with the club right through to the end, when they left for Arizona. The last time I spoke to him was over the winter, and even though he's pushing eighty, he's still pretty sharp. Lives over in Gifford, which is just up the road from Vero. I'm sure he'll welcome the opportunity to talk to someone about the old times. Let me give him a call. Question is, when could you talk to him? You guys are pretty busy during the day with your practice schedule."

"The boys have some downtime between the afternoon practice and dinner," said Crockett. "See if he's available then."

"Will do," said Burgos. "But listen, Darnell. I've got to kinda warn you about ol' Charlie. He can be a little cantankerous at times. But if you get on his good side right away, he'll be fine. And I got a hunch he'll take to you right off the bat."

"Great, thanks," I said.

Once that was out of the way, Crockett announced that we'd have live batting practice that afternoon for the first time. The guys, who were all tired of hitting in the cages against the JUGS machines, gave a round of applause, though I wasn't thrilled. Remember, I'd almost killed my coach the previous day. But even though the pitchers wouldn't be throwing full speed, Crocker pulled me aside and told me I'd be sitting this one out. A small part of me was disappointed and embarrassed, but to tell the truth, overall I was relieved.

So, while Trey and the other pitchers took turns feeding three-quarter meatballs to the guys, I threw on the side with all three catchers in between their practice hacks.

That it was my turn to hit, and as luck would have it, Trey was on the mound. So, I popped on a helmet, grabbed a bat, and stood in. Frankie Lammers, who was catching at that point, whispered, "Stay loose in there, Darnell," so that Trey couldn't hear him. Sure enough, Knight had a real laugh as I dug in. "Don't worry, man, I ain't gonna hit you are nothin'," he said. "Just tell me where you want it and I'll put it *exactly* there. I promise."

"Just throw the damn ball, man," I replied. So, he grooved one and I smacked it back up the middle, and he had to skip rope to get out of the way. His next pitch, which had a little more on it, I rifled at his head, and he had to duck or it would've decapitated him.

"Hey, Bro, I think he's trying to kill you," cracked Paco, who was on deck. "I wonder why?"

Well, this must've ticked off our resident prima

donna, because the next pitch came in chin-high and backed me out of there. "I thought you could put it anywhere I wanted!" I yelled at him, picking up my batting helmet, which had flown off.

"Oops, sorry, that one got away from me," he snickered.

So he grooved the next one like he was supposed to—but almost full speed—and I put it into orbit, a real monster shot. And since we always ran out the last swing of our set, I Cadillaced it around the bases while he glowered at me. I figured we were now even. But when he yelled, "Know what? You hit like an outfielder!" I snapped and took off in his direction, determined to lay him out. But before I even got three steps, Paco had tackled me from behind. Of course, the rest of the guys and the coaches came running up, and Crockett was livid.

"I can't believe what I'm seeing!" he yelled, the veins popping out on his neck. "Have you two knuckleheads lost your minds?"

Trey managed a "But—" before Crockett let him have it. "First of all, Mr. Knight, you've been riding Hayward's butt from the moment we got down here. I'm sick and tired of hearing your wiseass remarks! The whole idea is to *support* your teammates, not tear them down! I'm surprised he didn't go after you sooner."

Then he turned to me. "And you, Darnell, did the worst thing in my book. You showed up a teammate, which we *never* do around here. What am I always saying? *Respect the game!* That better be the last time I see *anybody* on this team Cadillac around the bases.

"Now, what I *should* do is send the both of you home, but that wouldn't be fair to your teammates, who are counting on you for Saturday. So why don't we do this: I want to two of you to start running, *side-by-side*, around this field, until I tell you to stop. I don't even want to *look* at you two right now. Get going!"

I got up and dusted myself off, but not before Paco said to Trey, "Hey, Bro, you owe me, man."

"What for?"

"For saving your life," he replied. "Next time you might not be so lucky."

So the two of us took off with our punishment jog and proceeded to run in silence for the next hour until the team went in. Neither of us would say he was sorry or try to make things any better. What can I tell you; we were seventeen.

* * *

That evening Joe Burgos was back during our dinner break with some news: Charlie Sutton was going to come over to Historic Dodgertown to meet with me on Friday after the afternoon practice. "Mr. Burgos," I said, "he doesn't have to do that. A phone conversation would've been okay."

"No, Darnell, he insisted," said Burgos. "Especially I told him a little about your background, and that you had a relative who'd been a ballplayer back in the day. He's glad you're taking an interest."

I felt it was okay to share this information with my teammates during dinner and told them about my grandfather. Jeez, a couple of the guys hadn't even *heard* of the Negro Leagues, much less the Monarchs… and we lived in Kansas City! Even Trey, who was keeping a low profile after our near dustup during practice, seemed interested.

"Look at you, the history buff," teased Paco as we pulled on our jogging stuff back at the villa. "'Bout time you took an interest in this. Just one thing, though. Why hasn't your granddad told you all about this stuff? You know, his time with the Monarchs, and coming to Dodgertown? Did something happen to him down here? Did he get hurt? Or did he just get cut from the club?"

"Well, he was only one of many guys invited to camp," I said. "Who knows what happened? You would think he would have at least been assigned to one of their minor league teams once they broke camp down here. But as far as I know, that never happened. Maybe he was too proud to go to the minors after having played at the top level of the Negro Leagues. I hope this Charlie guy can fill me in if he even remembers my grandfather."

"Hey, Bro, it's worth a shot. Let's get going. Time for me to work off that extra slice of apple pie I had. And I'll bet you can't wait to do a little more running. On the positive side, if the baseball thing doesn't work out, you and Trey can always go out for the track team."

"Very funny. We didn't say a word to each other the whole time we ran."

"Well, I wouldn't expect him to be eager to make nice with you. Even with all your problems down here, he considers you a threat. It's funny; he's got a great arm, movie star looks, girls all over him at school, and pro scouts looking at him already… but he's still the most insecure guy you're ever gonna meet. Talk about high maintenance. Anyway, I think the guys were happy you went after him. Crockett and Putney tolerate Trey because we need him to win, but as for the rest of us, I think they were hoping that I lost my grip on you for a second. To tell you the truth, I was thinking about it myself."

Chapter Eight
The Third Night

Not much happened during our evening jog around Dodgertown, but afterwards we got some welcome news from Coach Crockett: we'd be having an intrasquad scrimmage on Friday afternoon. Of course, that brought cheers from everyone, because even in beautiful weather you get sick of drills after a while.

So, again I waited till late when Paco was snoring away, put on a baseball undershirt and my game pants, grabbed my glove and spikes and trusty bag of baseballs, and tiptoed out. It was another gorgeous night, a little cooler than the last one and still pretty clear, although some clouds were creeping in. I found myself almost jogging towards the footbridge, I was so excited. In my haste, I did make one key decision. I figured if they thought I was my grandfather, and, if in their minds it was really 1953, then I would play along and become Willie Jackson. What would be the harm? PawPaw and I were both right-handed pitchers who were trying to make the team, and obviously, we looked a lot alike. But I was really nervous about trying to pass myself off as a guy from the '50s. Truth is, I was never much one for history—until that point, anyway. All I knew from my social studies classes about that era was that we were in a war in Vietnam—no, Korea—and that Eisenhower, the famous general from World War II, was president. Rock and roll music was just getting started, cars were big and clunky, and gas was cheap. As far as black folks were concerned, we basically had no rights, especially in the South. America seemed to be more concerned with fighting communism than with civil rights. Oh yeah, I also did a quick search on my phone and found that in 1952, the Brooklyn Dodgers had lost to the Yankees in the World Series, 4 games to 3. So that's all I knew about the time period I was going to try to fake my way through. And I thought I might be able to pull it off, because I was just a dumb high school kid who didn't know any better.

As promised, "Ed" and "Harold" had brought a third man with them, a rangy black guy who was decked out in a golf shirt and slacks. He seemed to have a strong upper torso, and his hair was short in the style of the day.

"Willie, this is Joe," said Harold. "He's a really fine pitcher and should be able to help you out some. If I were you, I'd listen to whatever he has to say."

I shook hands with the man—another icy grip—and immediately noticed the strength in his long fingers. "Hey, Willie, I'm Joe," he said. "Pleased to meet you."

"Same here," I said.

"Why don't you two go over to the pitching wall by yourselves, have a nice chat," said Ed. "Harold and I aren't pitchers anyway, so we'd just complicate things."

"Sounds good," said Joe in a gravelly baritone.

And so, Joe and I turned back and began our walk towards the wall near Field 3. I waited for him to start the conversation, but this time at least I had a heads-up, because when I'd looked up the '52-'53 Dodgers, I saw that they had a great pitcher named Joe Black, a righty like me, who'd won the 1952 Rookie of the Year Award. This had to be him.

"So you played for the Monarchs, huh?" he said in his low, rumbling voice, breaking the ice. "That's some organization. Buck O'Neil's a great manager, I hear."

"Uh-huh," I answered tentatively.

"Me, I started with the Baltimore Elite (he pronounced it ee-light) Giants, but I'm originally from Plainfield, New Jersey. Funny thing, Willie… I got to the Giants by a pure fluke. See, in Jersey I played on my high school team, and I was pretty good, too. But when the pro scouts came to watch us play, they paid no mind to me."

"How come?"

"Because I was a Negro. Man, I couldn't believe it. I was just about the best player on the team and they totally ignored me.

"So, I ended up going to Morgan State College in Maryland on scholarship to play baseball. That's a Negro school, you understand. Anyway, one of my teammates was Cal Irvin. His brother Monte plays for the Giants now, but back then he played for the Newark Eagles. It was Cal who suggested we go see a game between the Eagles and the Elite Giants." He laughed. "It was a shocking experience."

"How come?"

"Because stupid me didn't know there *was* such a thing as the Negro Leagues. Can you believe that?

"So anyway, Cal and I were sitting in the stands watching the game, and I guess we were a little loud when commenting on the talent of the Elite Giants players. Well, it just so happened that we were sitting in front of the Giants' owner, and he heard us. He probably thought we were a couple of smart alecks, but he asked us who we were anyway. When we told him we were ballplayers at Morgan State, he invited us to try out for the Giants."

"Did you go?"

"Oh, yeah. It was on a Tuesday. And would you believe that by Saturday I was in the starting lineup at shortstop against the New York Black Yankees?"

"Wow," I said. "That was quick."

"I'll say," he replied. "Thing was, I struck out three times. But when the manager wanted to drop me from the club, I explained to him that I was really a pitcher. So, I ended up sticking with the club. It was hard not to, because my first catcher with the Giants was Campy."

"Roy… Campanella?" I ventured, hoping I wasn't making a fool out of myself.

"One and the same. So, when the Dodgers went to scout Campy for the big club, they saw me, too, and eventually I got signed. But it took a while. You see, there was—and still is—an unwritten quota system in the Major Leagues. Even teams like the Dodgers, who were the first to do it, are hesitant to add Negroes unless they're really good. Many teams don't even have a single colored player yet. But that's how I got signed, anyway."

"That's some story," I said.

"Yeah, well, let's concentrate on you now." We'd reached the wall. "Tell me what you throw, Willie."

"Fastball, curve, and a changeup, though my change is kind of weak."

"Then why are you throwing it?"

"My coach thinks I need three pitches."

"Humph," he said. "Okay, so what's been the problem?"

"I've been really wild, and nobody can figure out why."

"All right, man," he said. "Get up on the mound and let's see your delivery."

"Okay." I proceeded to show him the no-windup motion they'd had me switch to last season.

"Uh-uh, I don't like that," said Joe. "You got to establish a rhythm, but that motion has you going all herky-jerky. Nossir, that won't do. Give me your glove and watch me." He scooped a ball out of the bag and toed the rubber, bending forward at the waist while staring at the strike zone square on the wall as he positioned the ball in the web of my glove. "First thing I do is bring my arms down at my sides and swing 'em way back behind me, like so… gets the rhythm started, see?"

"Uh-huh."

"Then I bring 'em forward, all the way up over my head, while I step back with my left foot; then I shift my weight to my back leg to get a nice high left leg kick and drive forward, so my right knee's almost scraping the ground as I come over the top during my release and follow-through." He'd demonstrated every step in slow motion as he talked. "So here's how it looks all together." He leaned forward, pretended to look in for the sign, then rocked back, his hands swinging up high over his head, before he drove towards the plate, his left foot pointed far forward as his right arm came over the top and flung the ball towards the wall. It hit the painted square with a pronounced *crack* that reverberated in the stillness of the night. "See?" he said. "One smooth motion. Now you try it, Willie."

I have to admit, I was a little hesitant. See, nowadays nobody uses a big windup like back in the day. That's because coaches feel it makes it easier for baserunners to steal a bag on you. But I was so desperate I would've stood on my head to throw strikes. Anyway, I did a slow test windup, and Joe nodded as I went from one stage to the next. Then he placed his right hand on my shoulder, and I swear there was a shock of electricity between us. "Okay, now, let's go full speed," he said, backing away. "Give me a fastball."

I cleared my mind, took a deep breath, blew it out, and did a one-two-three count to myself as I rocked back, wound up and delivered, my right knee ending up inches from the mound.

Strike.

"Do it again," said Joe.

Amazed at what I'd just accomplished, I grabbed another ball from the bag, rocked, kicked, and dealt.

Strike.

"Again."

Strike.

"Okay, now show me your curve," he said.

I nodded, wound up, and snapped off a beauty. My curve isn't a 12 to 6 sweeper, but it has a real bite if I throw it well. This time I did.

Strike.

Joe smiled in the moonlight, his dark face lit up by his white teeth. "You see, Willie?" he said. "You got a rhythm going. I can tell you're doing some kinda cadence to yourself, right?"

"Uh-huh."

"Well then, if that's what works for you, stay with it. And don't let anybody tell you otherwise, you got me?"

"Yeah."

"Okay, then. Waddya say we empty this whole bag and make sure you got it down?"

"Sure!"

And so I threw and threw, mixing fastballs and curves, working up a good sweat. Joe just kept nodding, offering an "uh-huh" or a comment here and there, and continuing to smile at my progress. I could've thrown for hours, but then there was a sudden rumble of distant thunder. I was so into what I was doing that I'd failed to notice how cloudy it had become.

"Let's gather these balls up and take cover in one of the dugouts," he said. "Sky's about to open up." So we threw them in the bag and hustled over to one of the covered benches at Practice Field 3 as lightning started cracking around us. "Might as well wait it out here," he said as it began pouring on Dodgertown. "Unless you're afraid of a little lightning."

"I'm okay," I said, feeling safe with this guy, like nothing could touch me.

"Good," said Joe. But I've gotta ask you, Willie, what's with your pants?"

"Huh?"

"You've got 'em pulled way down to your ankles, man. That's not the way big leaguers wear their uniform."

He had me. I mean, the style when I was in high school, and even today, is to wear your pants tight and nearly touching your spikes. I must've looked like a clown to him.

"What you want to do," he said, "is have them come down to around the calf, so your uniform stirrups can show. Some guys wear 'em a little higher, but you get the idea. If you want to be a Major Leaguer, you've gotta look the part."

"Okay," I said, tugging my pant legs up.

"And another thing," he added, eyeing me suspiciously. "What's that medallion around your neck? Some kinda religious thing?"

I brought my fingers up to the silver dollar-sized peace sign that was suspended by a leather string, the only thing I had left from my former girlfriend, who'd given it to me the previous Christmas. One thing that was positive about Vanessa, she was all into the whole peace and love philosophy. But how could I explain to this guy from 1953 a symbol that wouldn't become known until well into the 1960s? All I could come up with was, "Uh, my girlfriend made it for me."

Joe shrugged. "Oh, it's like that. Well, that's fine, Willie. Just looks a little odd, is all." He looked out through the pouring rain at the practice diamonds and sighed. "You know," he said, "last year I won 15 games, all of them in relief, and had 15 saves. You see, we were a little short on pitching at the beginning of the season, with Don Newcombe being in the service, so our manager, Charlie Dressen, gave me a shot, and I just kept doing the job. Man, we had a great ballclub—still do. So we got to the World Series against the Yanks, and you know what Dressen did?"

"What?"

"He was so confident in me that he had me *start* three games in the Series. Can you believe that?"

"How'd you do?"

"Well, I beat 'em 4-2 in the opener. Imagine that. I was the first Negro starting pitcher to win a World Series game. I remember they had both teams line up on the baselines at Ebbets Field before the first game for the National Anthem, and I'm looking across at the Yankees, and there wasn't a single colored face on that club… but we had Jackie and Campy and me, and all I could think was *God bless America*. Here it was, my boyhood dream back in New Jersey, to be in a World Series, and I was starting Game One! You might think I was nervous, that it was a lot for the club to put on my shoulders. But instead, a kind of serenity came over me. Man, there was *no way* those Yankees were beating me that day.

"The other two starts, I barely lost... I mean, I was taken out in one of 'em in the 8th inning leading 1-0. We just didn't hit real good against the Yanks' pitchers. My ERA that season was 2.15, and in the Series it was 2.50. Not bad for a rookie, Willie."

"I'll say," I said, figuring that in modern times those stats would get him a multi-million-dollar contract.

"Now," he continued, "do you know why my teammates play hard for me?"

"How come?"

"Because they know I'll protect them. Last year the New York Giants' pitchers tried to intimidate our guys, threw a lot of inside pitches. Know what I did? Knocked down like five of their guys in a row. When those Giants saw I meant business, they laid off our batters." He smiled at the memory and gave one of those low chuckles.

I said, "Can I tell you something, Joe?"

"Sure."

"Right now, I'm the only Black—uh, Negro—in my, uh, group down here. Sometimes it kind of gets to me, you know?"

"What, do you mean you're nervous about guys on the other teams ragging on you from the dugout?"

"Well, yeah, though at times I even have to wonder about some of my own teammates. I mean, being accepted and all."

Joe continued to stare at the field; the rain seemed to be letting up a bit. "I'm not going to say it's been easy for me, Willie," he said. "I've been called some pretty nasty things from the other dugouts, but you know what? In the end, they've still gotta get in the batter's box and face me, and I've got a very hard ball in my hand, you dig?"

"Yeah."

"Of course, when I got here, I had Jackie and Campy and Newk to back me up. But can you imagine what it was like for Jackie when he was the only one? That took more guts than I can imagine. It was bad enough that he had to deal with the bigots on the other team, but there was some dissension here too, until Pee Wee and some of the other guys got it straightened out.

"As far as your teammates are concerned, once you prove yourself as a player, they'll *have* to accept you. And if they don't, that's their loss. What I'm saying is, you can't let it get to you. From what I can see, you've got great stuff. All you need is self-confidence. But another thing is, don't let people mess with your style, if you think what you're doing is right. This year in camp they're trying to get me to throw a screwball and a big curve, when I got along just fine with two pitches last year. And I'm afraid it's gonna mess me up. Maybe it's because they want to convert me to a fulltime starter this year, I don't know." He sighed. "Then again, they do pay my salary, and if I refuse to listen to them, there's always some guy like you in the minors who would like to come take my place." He shot me a sly grin.

"Anyway," he concluded, "all I can tell you, Willie, is that you just have to concentrate on what you do best, rear back and let it fly. Can you remember that?"

"Sure."

The rain had stopped now, and fat droplets were falling intermittently from the dugout's overhang. "That's what I love about the rain down here," said Joe.

"It can come down really hard, but if you're patient, it eases off. You get what I'm saying?"

"Yeah."

Joe turned to me and smiled. "Say, Willie. The guys told me to tell you—if you did good tonight—that they want you to come back again tomorrow, and to bring a bat, too."

"A bat? Why?"

"You'll find out. But please, fix those pants, okay?"

"Sure, Joe. Thanks for everything tonight."

"No problem." He stood up and stretched. "Gotta head back," he said, pointing towards the bridge. "Keep working hard, Willie. Okay?"

"You know it."

I sat there as he walked away, the grass *squish-squishing* under his shoes, until he faded in the darkness.

Chapter Nine
Day Four

At breakfast the next day I was bursting with mixed emotions. On the one hand, I had pitched better under the watchful eye of Joe Black than I had in over a year. Clearly, I had pretty much total control over both my fastball and curve. And, despite all the throwing, I wasn't feeling any soreness at all. I attributed it to the fluidity with which I was working.

But there was also something nagging at me. While it was one thing to pitch in the company of only one person, even if he was only a spirit or ghost or whatever, it would be a whole different deal to do it in broad daylight with my coaches and teammates looking on.

Or, more disturbingly, had I imagined the whole thing with Joe Black, and was I really cracking up? If I went out there today and threw the ball all over the place, what could that signify? That I really *was* a head case?

Now that I was officially back with the pitchers, I was more anxious to see what would happen during our morning session at the practice mounds. Today, Frankie Lammers, our second-string catcher, was to be my battery mate. As we jogged over to the practice mounds after the team stretch, I told him I'd be trying out a new windup. He said that was fine but asked if the coaches knew about this. Remember, it was they who'd had me go to a no-windup delivery. So, I pulled Coach Putney aside while the catchers were strapping on their gear.

"Really? What prompted this, Darnell?" he asked nonchalantly, though his face was pretty concerned.

"Just a feeling, Coach," I said. "I'd like to try it out today, if you don't mind."

"Be my guest," he said. "But start off slow, so I can really check it out."

"You got it."

Well, it didn't take long for the other guys to pick up on the fact that the team head case was now adopting a style from a bygone era. "What in the world are you *doing*, man?" asked Trey from a couple mounds away. "This isn't the 1920s!" Even Paco had tipped his mask back on his protective helmet and was eyeing me suspiciously.

Fortunately, Frankie was game for whatever I had in mind, and went into his squat. Behind me stood Coach Putney, staring intently, his hands on his knees. Finally, after a few real slow windups for his benefit, I nodded to Frankie that I was ready. It was the coolest morning of the week, but I was sweating bullets.

I wish I could tell you that I really lit it up that first day after Joe had worked with me, but the results were mixed at best. While it's true that I didn't throw the ball five feet high or wide of Frankie's glove, I wasn't exactly attacking the strike zone, either. And I bounced a few of my curveballs. So, although Putney didn't just stop me right there and tell me to trash the new delivery, he did suggest I stay at three-quarter speed until I had some sort of handle on it. Again, I felt embarrassed that our other pitchers were humming the ball while I was throwing like some guy rehabbing a bad arm.

On the way to lunch, Paco said, "Saw the new windup routine. You gonna stay with it?"

"I don't know," I said, the doubts creeping back in. "What do you think?"

"Listen, *amigo*," he replied, "all I know is this: We have an intrasquad game coming up tomorrow, and you're gonna want to pitch in that if you want to have any chance of pitching against Vero Beach on Saturday. So the way I see it, you got about 24 hours to figure it out, Bro."

One positive that afternoon was that Coach Crockett, who'd been clued in by Putney about my new delivery, let me take a turn throwing live BP. And I did okay, though it was only half-speed. However, I still couldn't groove it pitch after pitch like the other guys, and I could hear some of our hitters, their voices lowered, griping amongst themselves after they took their swings against me.

At dinner that night, Crockett got a round of cheers for announcing that this evening we'd have our final team jog. He also said that he'd be splitting the roster with Coach Putney for tomorrow's intrasquad game, and that some pitchers might have to play the field to round out the lineups, or maybe even play for both squads, as we didn't have quite enough guys to field two teams.

As usual, my teammates had spent the hour or so after the afternoon practice frolicking around in the pool, even though today had been on the cool side. I just sat around the room and read up a little more on the Brooklyn Dodgers, wondering what I was in for later that night. But you know, when I was reading, something dawned on me that afternoon. As I researched the Brooklyn Dodgers, I saw that, except maybe the Yankees, more had been written about those teams than anyone else. I mean, everybody in my school knew who Jackie Robinson was, but Joe Black? Duke Snider and Pee Wee Reese? I had no clue. Which, I guess, was the only thing stopping me from believing I had only been imagining these guys the past couple nights. And then I remembered reading an article in a sports magazine saying that some black players in the *Majors* didn't even know who Robinson was, at least until they retired his number all across baseball back in the '90s. So as I lay there, I made a promise to myself that if I ended up staying with baseball, I was going to learn everything I could about the game and its history, including the story of its black players.

Of course, that led me to another question: Why had my grandfather, who'd played with one of the most famous Negro League teams and even had a tryout with the Brooklyn Dodgers, never shared his experiences with his grandson who had taken up the game? What exactly had happened to the guy to turn him off so bad? I was going to find out, no matter what it took, whether I continued playing baseball or not.

But I had bigger problems at the moment. Like for example, were my teammates giving up on me? When Paco got back from the pool I asked if there had been any comments about my BP session, and he said, "Not really," but I knew he was lying. I just let it go, but I realized it was time for me to put up or shut up.

And so, as we were gathering at dusk for that last team run, I was ready when Crockett sidled over to me. I dreaded what was coming when he began with, "Now Darnell, about tomorrow's intrasquad game—"

"I'd really like to pitch, Coach," I said in a preemptive strike.

"You would?"

"Yessir." There, I'd done it.

"Okay," he said. "Then what I'll do is split up you and Trey. He's starting for my squad, and you'll be the second pitcher into the game for Coach Putney's team." I think he could see the disappointment in my eyes, so he quickly added, "But, if you have a good outing, I'll definitely work you in there against Vero Beach on Saturday."

"When it counts, or just for mopping up?" I asked, immediately regretting my boldness.

"That'll depend on how you look tomorrow. Listen, Darnell, next week the season begins. I have to set my rotation, and both of the juniors have really improved from last year. In a perfect world, you and Trey would be my top two starters. But you've gotta show me something, son."

"I understand," I said. "Sorry I mouthed off, Coach."

"Nobody wants to see you succeed more than me, Darnell," he replied. "Heck, I *want* my players to be aggressive. Just give me your best effort and I'll be satisfied, no matter how it turns out. I'll be rooting for you." And with that, he blew his whistle, and we all took off on our last team jog around Dodgertown.

Chapter Ten
The Fourth Night

That night I waited Paco out, as usual, and crept out of the villa. But I hadn't gone five steps from the door when I remembered that Joe had said to bring a bat this time. Cursing my forgetfulness, I snuck back in and gently eased one of Paco's bats out of his carry bag. I almost died when it clinked against another bat and he turned over. But my roomie was a deep sleeper, and he never stopped snoring.

My heart was beating a mile a minute as I speed-walked past the practice fields, lugging the ball bag and bat, and headed towards the footbridge. Unlike the previous night, there was no threat of rain, which was a plus. However, showers were in the forecast for the next day. I hoped this wouldn't wipe out the intrasquad game, but that wasn't as important as the here and now, and I forced myself to focus as I passed the swishing palm trees that lined the paved golf cart paths.

Even from a distance I could see that Duke, Pee Wee and Joe were waiting for me, and I checked myself to make sure I'd hiked up my pant legs like Joe had suggested. Thank goodness Coach Crockett required us all to wear black spikes. I can't imagine what Joe would've said if I showed up in white or multicolored ones, like a lot of teams were wearing at the time.

So I stepped onto the bridge, and then it hit me—How was I going to explain the aluminum bat slung over my shoulder? Or at least, it had been when I'd left the villa. Because *the bat I was now carrying was a Louisville Slugger made of white ash*. No lie.

"'Bout time, Willie," said Pee Wee in that Southern drawl of his. "Ready for a workout?"

"You know it," I said. "Are we going back to the pitching wall?"

"Not tonight," said Duke coolly. "We're going somewhere else."

"We are?"

"Yeah," said Joe. "I think it's time you get a look at the inside of Holman Stadium. It's brand-new, you know. Come on."

So I shrugged and followed behind the three men, but here's the thing: the aluminum bat turning wooden was freaky enough; but then, the second the three of them stepped off the other side of the bridge, they were wearing their home white Brooklyn uniforms, with *Dodgers* scripted across the front in blue and their number in red underneath. Their metal spikes *clackety-clacked* on the paved path. But still, they never acknowledged the transformation of their attire; it was like this was *supposed* to happen. I just kept following them towards the ballpark, too amazed to utter a word.

Holman Stadium was bordered on the right-hand side by a deep row of luxurious six-foot hedges. Behind these hedges were positioned medium-height palm trees every ten yards or so. We passed through the ground-level entrance down the right field line where there was a break in the hedges, and I saw the inside of this beautiful old-time park for the first time. The field itself was in kind of a recessed bowl, with single-tier grandstands rising above it. The stands reached to the ends of the outfield fence down the baselines, and there was a grassy berm beyond the centerfield fence. Towering palm trees had been planted on top of the berm. A small press box sat atop the stands behind the chain-link backstop. I just stood there, gaping. And then, no joke, the light towers began flickering and then came on, bathing the field in a yellowish glow.

"Come on, Willie," said Pee Wee. "There's a couple more guys waiting on us at home plate."

So again, I fell in line behind the Dodger trio, but it wasn't long before the identity of the other two was clear. On this night in Vero Beach in the year 2012, Jackie Robinson and Roy Campanella, their creamy white uniforms in contrast with their dark faces, were chatting and having a leisurely warm-up catch.

Robinson, the darker of the two, was the first to notice me. "So, Pee Wee, you brought the rook with you?" he said in a high-pitched, mocking tone.

"Ease off, Jack," chirped Campanella jovially. "You're gonna frighten the boy half to death." Then they both came over and shook my hand, which was shaking already.

"Jack Robinson," said #42 as he grasped mine. "Glad to have you with us."

"Thanks," I said, trying not to hyperventilate.

"Same with me, even though you're a Monarch," joked the powerfully built catcher, his skin as frigid as Robinson's. Then he turned serious. "The fellas here tell us you're having some control problems," he said. "Onliest way to straighten that out just to have you do some live pitchin'. Mr. Rickey's strings can only accomplish so much."

I had no idea what the string thing was about, but I did understand what "live" meant. Was I actually going to *pitch* to these guys? Then I figured, *Of course you are, dummy. Why do you think Joe said to bring a bat?*

"What say we warm up a bit?" suggested Snider. "Willie brought a whole bag of balls."

"Yeah, why not?" said Reese, dipping in his hand for one. And then, the three guys I walked in with did something I'd never seen before: They reached around to their back pockets and pulled out their gloves, which had been folded up inside! It was a good thing I favored a small glove myself, unlike the huge baskets some of my teammates wore, or the Dodgers would've been giving me the eye. I guessed that was the custom back in the day.

So, we formed two lines facing each other and paired off: Campanella and Reese, Snider and Black, and me and Jackie Robinson. I was having a catch with *Jackie Robinson.* It was all I could do to not drop the ball when he zipped it at me with a distinct *snap* that sent it straight as a string to my breastbone. But I fought off the jitters and managed to toss it right back to him. The other guys were chit-chatting, and I really wanted to listen in—I mean, what do ghosts talk about, right? But I concentrated on the man across from me.

"So, did you like being with the Monarchs, Willie?" he said, studying my face.

"It was all right," I replied, playing along. "And Buck O'Neil's a fine manager. Treated me real well."

"Yeah," he said, "Buck's a good man. But you don't want to be riding those buses anymore, Willie. Besides, the Negro Leagues are dying a slow death, now that more of us are making it to the big leagues. In another ten years at most they'll be finished, just you watch. And that's a good thing."

I wasn't about to disagree with him. Man, he had this intense glare that was plain scary. I also made a mental note to research this Buck O'Neil guy, as everybody—including me now—was talking him up so much.

"Everybody warm?" asked Reese after a couple minutes. "Or how about a game of Pepper?"

"Sure," said Jackie. "I'll hit."

"I had a feeling he'd say that," cracked Snider.

Again, it was panic time for me. What on earth was *Pepper*?

I was soon to find out. Robinson grabbed the bat, and I backed up, mimicking the other guys, to about 15 feet away, so we faced him in a line, a yard or so apart. Suddenly, Reese whipped a ball at Jackie, and he rapped it on the ground to Black, who deftly gloved it and threw it right back at him, rapid-fire style. And so it went for a few hectic minutes. Luckily for me, I fielded all my chances cleanly and returned the ball instantly. Jackie really was enjoying himself, making the grounders sharper and more difficult as we went along.

I can't begin to tell you what it was like to be among those guys as they laughed, joked, and ragged on each other. I had to keep reminding myself that these men weren't just legends, they were people from different walks of life who came together in a different time from mine, a difficult time, and somehow managed to get along and reach a level of excellence that few teams ever could. As far as I was concerned that ghostly game of Pepper could have lasted forever. It was the most fun in athletics that I've ever had. But it was not to be, as the game finally ended when Campanella booted one.

"C'mon, Camp," teased Robinson. "These should be easier for you, being you're built so low to the ground."

"Not with wearing a catcher's glove, they ain't!" he shot back, and everyone laughed.

I wondered why I had never heard of this simple game; but then again, there was so much about baseball, I realized, that I didn't know or appreciate. But I tell you what, I was gonna make it become a part of future practices with my teammates.

"Okay, let's get down to business," said the captain. "Duke, you go to the outfield and shag, and I'll take your relays on the infield. Joe, you stand near Willie and observe while he throws to Campy. And Jack, would you do us the honor of standing in against Willie?"

"With pleasure," he said in that high-pitched voice of his. "But only if I get to swing eventually."

"Deal," said Reese. "But let him just throw a couple by you first. To get the range, you understand."

"Uh-huh."

Joe plunked down the ball bag to the side of the mound and took his place behind it to keep an eye on me, and Campy turned his hat around, pounded his glove, and squatted behind the plate. "Let's keep it simple, Willie," he said. "One for a fastball, a deuce for the curve."

"Okay… Campy," I said, trying to control my breathing as the right-handed Robinson stepped into the batter's box, assuming a wide stance and holding the bat high. *Here goes*, I thought.

Campanella put down a single digit, and I nodded. Then, I went into the deliberate full windup Joe had taught me and let it fly, but it kind of got away from me, boring in on Robinson so that he had to jackknife backwards.

"Hee hee!" cackled Campy. "Stay loose in there, Jack! This boy's got a live one!"

"S-sorry," I mumbled in Robinson's direction.

He stepped out of the box and glared at me. "*What* did you say to me?" he practically shrieked in that shrill voice of his.

"I said I was—"

"You *never* say that!" he yelled. "If you want to pitch for the Dodgers, you've gotta think you *own* this batter's box. If that takes backing me out of there, you *do* it. That's how baseball is played, son. Didn't they teach you that on the Monarchs? You want to last in this game, you gotta pitch with a mean streak. Do it again!" He dug in and raised the bat, glowering at me. Campy called for another fastball, and this one—by design, this time— came in even tighter, barely missing Jackie's chin. He didn't even flinch.

"Now Willie," drawled Reese from somewhere behind me, "we appreciate you taking Jack's advice, but that doesn't mean you have to *kill* him. Then we'd have to break in a new second baseman."

I had to suppress a chuckle, and when I looked toward the plate again, Robinson was allowing himself a grin. Then, in an instant the smile was gone, and it was back to business. "Bring it, Rook," he challenged. "From now on I'm swinging."

"Game on," I whispered to myself. And for the next five minutes, I battled Jackie Robinson.

Now, I'd like to tell you that I had #42 flailing at my pitches, that he couldn't hit my heater with a paddle, but that wasn't the case. Yeah, I got a couple by him, and he fouled off a few more, which made Campy cackle even more and got Jackie more irritated. But for the most part,

Jackie was on everything I threw, and rocketed shots all over the place. Poor Duke was getting a workout running them down before relaying them to Pee Wee, who subsequently rolled them back to Joe before he tossed them in the ball bag. So, yeah, Jackie Robinson owned me—but that wasn't important. Because what was happening was, I was in the strike zone on nearly every pitch. I got into a rhythm and just *pounded* the strike zone. And that death-ray glare from Jackie made me focus even more and keep coming at him. Finally, after launching one over the left field fence, he dropped the bat and said, "That's enough, man. I'm bushed. That okay with you, Rook?"

"Yeah," I said, pretty tired myself.

As I helped Joe scoop the last few scattered baseballs into the bag, the others gathered around the mound. "So, what's the verdict, Camp?" said Reese, hands on his hips.

"He's got good enough stuff for a kid," answered the catcher. "Needs a little polish, but I see a lot of promise. How about you, Jack?"

"He's got potential," allowed Robinson. "Could use a little more break on his curve, but he made me work."

"Me too!" quipped Snider, and they all laughed.

Then Jackie said, "Hey Duke, Pee Wee… give the three of us a minute with the kid."

"Sure thing," said the captain with a wink. "We'll see you back at the bridge, Willie." They started walking towards the right field grandstand exit.

"Okay, time to talk," said Robinson when the other two were out of earshot. "You showed us a lot tonight, kid," he began. "You've got all the tools. But there's more to it than that, Willie. As a Negro ballplayer, you can't just be as good as everybody else. You've got to rise above the others and be *special*. Same for me, Campy and Joe. Because there are those who are going to doubt you have what it takes, and I mean your head and your heart."

"That's happened to you, right?" said Black, recalling our conversation of the previous night. "Even with your own teammates?"

"Uh-huh," I said.

"That's the point, Willie," said Jackie. "You were nervous facing me tonight, and that's okay, because fear of the unknown can sometimes be a great motivator. But even though you were scared, you still knew I'm a guy who's on your side. Now, in the future you're gonna have to face other guys who want to destroy you out there, and there's gonna be pressure on you to perform. But you know what I believe? I think that pressure is a *privilege*. That's right, a privilege, because only people who want to achieve great things will find themselves in situations where it's all on their shoulders. So you've got to take that little bit of fear and make it work for you, believe in yourself, and count on your teammates to back you up. That's what we do on the Dodgers. Right, Camp?"

"Yup," said the catcher.

"All day long," added Joe Black.

"Anyway, training camp is ending soon," concluded Robinson. "You've just gotta make sure you keep your sights set on success and don't let anything, *or anybody*, stop you. And if you can do this, Willie… someday, maybe someday soon, you'll be a Dodger." He stuck out his cold, sweaty hand and I shook it; Campanella and Black followed suit.

"Thanks, fellas," I said. "I'll do my best, I promise."

"All right then," said Jackie to the others. "Time to

hit the showers." They turned and walked towards an exit on the far side of the park, and I picked up the bag of balls and the bat and went out the way I'd come in as the lights of Holman Stadium winked off one by one.

When I reached the bridge, Duke and Pee Wee were waiting for me, back in their street clothes. "Did you get your lecture from Jack?" chided Reese, an impish grin creasing his face.

"Oh, yeah," I said.

"He's pretty intense," said Snider. "But that's what makes him the player he is. I'm just glad he's on my team."

"Amen," said Reese. "Well, I guess this is good night, Willie. And I hope we've helped y'all out a bit. Time will tell. Best of luck to you." Then, for the last time I shook hands with the Duke of Flatbush and the Captain. They stood on the footbridge, waving goodbye as I pointed myself towards the practice fields and began walking, Paco's aluminum bat resting on my shoulder.

Chapter Eleven
The Fifth Day

Friday morning I woke up around six and immediately pulled back the drapes on the villa's window. It was raining. Not hard, but steady enough to dampen my spirits. I was really looking forward to the intrasquad game that afternoon, but now it was in jeopardy. And, without a good performance in the intrasquad, it was unlikely I'd get to pitch against Vero Beach the following day. So, I wasn't feeling too great. But it was about to get worse because, when I turned away from the window, my roommate was propped up on one elbow, studying me.

"Morning," I said.

"So, you want to tell me where you've been going at night, Bro?" he replied, an eyebrow raised suspiciously.

"W-what?" I stuttered.

"Don't try to play me, Bro," he said. "The last couple nights you've been sneaking out, and don't deny it. What you been up to? You got a girl down here or something?"

"No, no, nothing like that," I said. I was obviously busted, and I didn't really know how to explain this. What I *did* know was that I couldn't tell him the truth. Paco was probably the only guy on the team at this point who didn't think I was a nut job, and the last thing he wanted to hear was that I was hanging around with a bunch of dead Dodgers. "I-I've been working on things," I said.

"What things?"

"Pitching stuff… you know."

"Like that funky new windup?"

"Well… yeah."

He frowned at me. "Well, then why didn't you ask me to help you?" he said, a little hurt. "You know I would've helped you."

"I know," I said, "but it was something I kinda had to work out for myself. Besides, you're dead tired from catching all day. It would be unfair to drag you out there with me in the middle of the night."

"But isn't it like, *dark* out there? What could you get accomplished in the dark?"

Again, I couldn't explain how it just magically lightened up when the guys were working with me at the wall, or how the lights at Holman Stadium just happened to turn on when we set foot on the field. "It wasn't easy," I said as confidently as I could manage. "Lucky for me, the moon was out most of the time."

But Paco was no dummy, and he was still giving me the eye. "You know, I almost followed you out last night," he admitted. "I heard my bats rattling and that woke me up. Now, I can understand you going somewhere, maybe the practice mounds or that pitching wall we never use, to work on your motion. But why would you need a *bat*, man?"

"It's kinda hard to explain," I said. "Listen, Paco, maybe I was just wasting my time. But if it all works out, I promise I'll tell you all about it someday. You just have to trust me on this one." I decided to change the subject. "Hey, you think we'll get to play this afternoon?"

"Hope so," he said, stretching. "I'm sure Crockett will tell us what's what at breakfast. I'm gonna go take a shower and wake myself up. You don't know how great it's been having to share a bathroom with only one person." He padded off to the bathroom and I heaved a sigh of relief, wondering if he bought any of what I'd told him.

Jeez, I wasn't sure I believed it myself.

* * *

Of course, at breakfast everyone was buzzing about the weather; it was by far the most chilly day of the week, and the rain showers kept coming. We'd had to skirt the puddles on the cart paths to the conference center. But once we were all seated and chowing down, Coach Crockett put our fears to rest.

"Okay, gentlemen," he said, "listen up. According to the weather reports, this front is gonna pass over and be out of here by noon. Hopefully, the sun will come out and dry out the diamonds. Joe Burgos has assured me that as soon as it stops, the grounds crew will get on it and make the field playable. So, this morning we'll just take team batting practice in the indoor cages. Any questions?"

Trey put up his hand, and Crockett nodded at him. "Coach, have the rosters been set for the intrasquad game yet if we do end up playing?" he asked.

"That'll be finished by lunchtime," he replied patiently. "No need to be worrying about that now. Have faith in us, Trey. We'll manage to get you in there." That drew some laughs from the seniors, including Paco. I tried my hardest not to join in, but it was tough.

So after we finished eating, it was off to the cages, which were well-lit and carpeted in Astroturf. There were three of them, side-by-side, all of which were equipped with a JUGS machine. As always, there was good-natured ribbing as we took turns getting our hacks.

Now, we had some pretty good hitters on our team. The Bourke twins, our double-play combo, could spray the ball to all fields. "Dirt Devil" Pastorello had real power, as did Igor. And our outfielders, led by Mercury Mears, could really drive the ball into the power alley gaps and stretch singles into doubles. However, outside of Paco, our catchers couldn't hit much, especially Babe. Whenever he got into the cage, the ragging was brutal. Of course, Trey was the main culprit, but he had no business ragging on anyone, as he was a pretty pathetic hitter himself. However, when somebody got on his monstrous whiffs that morning, he was ready with an answer: "If you hammerheads haven't noticed," he declared, "the only place where pitchers still hit is the National League. Colleges and the minors use this designated hitter. And by the time I make it to the Majors, the NL will go to the DH, too. So what's the difference?"

Remarks like this would always have Crockett and Putney exchanging disgusted glances, but they couldn't get on him too much, as he was the ace of the staff. They'd just tell Trey to concentrate on his bunting and leave it at that.

As usual, I was the best hitter of the pitching staff. Besides Trey, who was a waste, our two lefties, Timmy Galvin and Rick Sages, could manage an occasional hit and move runners along with a well-placed bunt; but I was the only guy who might be called upon to pinch-hit in a tight game, and I was proud of that. Still, I wouldn't get too cocky about it because I'd then have Trey calling me a closet outfielder. So I just took my cuts and kept my mouth shut.

By the time we sat down for lunch, the rain had let up and the grounds crew was already raking the infield of Practice Field 1 in preparation for the intrasquad game while laying down this stuff called Diamond Dust to soak up any standing water. Crockett read off the lineups for the scrimmage, and there were no real surprises. As expected, Trey would go the first four innings for squad #1, managed by Crockett, and Paco would be his catcher; Galvin would then finish up. As for my team, Sages would go the first four, followed by me, with Frankie Lammers and Babe sharing the catching duties. It wasn't an ideal situation, but my performance so far had been spotty at best, and Rick deserved to start ahead of me.

As we were walking over to the field, the sun broke through, and I thought back to Joe Black's comment about the storm always passing at Dodgertown. I hoped that would apply to me this day. Scanning the small portable bleachers of Field 1, I saw Joe Burgos in attendance, as well as Amanda Lisnow, her medical kit at the ready. She looked at me and pointed to her right arm as if to say, "Everything okay?" and I gave her a thumbs-up.

No excuses now. It was time to play.

* * *

We broke up into two teams, and Coach Putney had our squad jog over to the far reaches of the outfield for stretching and warm-ups. But then I had an idea. Once we were done with that, I gathered a few guys who were

105

playing catch and took them aside. I grabbed a bat and said, "Who wants to play a little Pepper?" Of course, they looked at me like I was crazy.

"What's that?" said Igor.

"I'll show you." I lined up the four guys as the Dodgers had done the previous night and instructed them to feed me the ball. After a couple minutes of me hitting, somebody else took a turn, and so on. The other guys on my squad saw us and came over, wanting to join in. Soon we had *two* groups playing and laughing.

"Wow," said Putney, "I haven't seen anyone play Pepper since I was in Little League."

A few seconds later, Crockett left his squad and jogged over. "Can't believe what I'm watching," he marveled. "Who got this Pepper game going?"

"Darnell," said Putney.

"Where'd you learn about Pepper?" asked Crockett, obviously impressed.

"Oh, some friends of my grandfather," I replied with a smile.

* * *

Putney made the lineup for our squad, hitting me third, and asked if I would start the game in right field. "Just don't overdo it too much," he cautioned. "You're pitching the last three innings, remember."

"Sure thing, Coach," I said.

So, our team had a couple of soph subs at third and second, Bobby Bourke at short, Igor at first, another soph in left, Mercury in center and me in right, with Babe starting out behind the dish. I thought we had a slight advantage, although Crockett's team had Dirt Devil, both our starting corner outfielders, the other Bourke, and Paco catching. And, of course, our pitching ace, Trey.

We had first ups, and Trey quickly got our first two guys out. I made solid contact, but Tommy Lyons, one of our regular starters, tracked my drive and ran it down in left center. Three up, three down, and Trey strutted off the mound.

Rick Sages, our lefty starter, didn't fare as well. By the time the inning was over we were down three runs.

My squad came to life in the second inning and scratched out a run with some good situational hitting; but I have to admit, Trey looked overpowering.

I got up again an inning later—after Sages had given up two more runs—and smoked one over the third base bag for a double, which Trey wasn't too happy about. So, the next time he was up, he decided to really concentrate and cracked one up the right center alley. I hustled over and was just getting to the ball when I saw him turn first out of the corner of my eye. Clearly, he was challenging my arm.

Bad idea.

I came up throwing and pegged a perfect strike to Bourke as Trey slid into second. "Out!" yelled Crockett, who was umpiring the bases from behind the pitching mound.

"*What*?! You've gotta be kidding, Coach!" Trey whined. "I was in there!"

"'Fraid not," said Crockett. "Have a seat, son."

Trey looked out at me, and I just mimed a pistol with my throwing hand, pulled the trigger, and blew on my barrel finger. It was pretty sweet.

Anyway, by the time it was my turn to pitch they had us in a hole, 5-2. The score didn't matter. All eyes were on me as I took the mound. "Nice and easy, Darnell," said Putney, who was calling balls and strikes from behind the plate. I took my warmup tosses and signaled that I was ready as Dirt Devil Pastorello dug into the batter's box. And then, for some inexplicable reason, I did something I'd never done before. I took the peace medallion out from under my shirt and kissed it before putting it back. Don't ask me why.

"Right here, Darnell!" said Frankie, who put down the fastball sign and gave me the target. I nodded, went into my new windup… and threw a perfect strike, which Pastorello took.

"Attaboy, Darnell!" said Putney, and I heaved a huge sigh of relief. *Hey*, I said to myself, *if you could pitch to Jackie Robinson, these guys should be a piece of cake*. And they were. I mean, nobody could *touch* me. Frankie mixed in curves with my fastball, and I was constantly around the plate. A couple guys managed feeble ground balls, but they were quickly gobbled up for easy outs. And Trey? He almost corkscrewed himself into the ground trying to make contact. Paco had the only hit against me, a bleeder up the middle, but I left him stranded on first. I'd never pitched better in my life. Basically, I'd held the line for our team, and we scored a few runs off Trey's successor, Galvin, to make it close at the end.

As I walked off the mound after my last inning, I could hear Putney crowing about my stuff to Crockett, who was beaming. I didn't catch all of what they were saying, but I did make out, "Looks like we got our pitcher back."

The coaches gathered the whole team together and sat us down in the outfield. "Guys, that was a great effort," said Crockett. "Coach Putney and I really liked what we saw today. I think we're gonna be just fine this season"— he looked directly at me—"and tomorrow we'll get to measure ourselves against a good team. Vero Beach High School is a perennial power in this area. They're also the biggest school around, and they have a fairly larger student population than us. But fellas, it still comes down to the nine people we're gonna run out there, and based on what I saw today, you guys can stack up against anybody."

Of course, we all whooped it up over that.

"As for tomorrow," he continued, "we've got a doubleheader, two 7-inning games, beginning at 1:30 PM. So, tomorrow morning after breakfast, I want you guys to just relax in your rooms. We'll do a light lunch, and head over to Holman Stadium together for pregame warm-ups at one. Any questions?"

Predictably, Trey put his hand up. "What are the lineups, Coach?" he asked, which really meant, "Am I starting game one?"

"Coach Putney and I will figure all that out by tomorrow. Everybody will get some innings. Remember, we've got two games to play, and it's supposed to be a warm day. So make sure you guys start hydrating tomorrow morning." He looked at his watch. "It's still a little cool, but, if you want to go to the pool for a little while now, that's up to you. We'll see you at dinner. Again, good job today."

We broke up and headed back towards the villas, but before I knew it, Crockett had eased over and was walking beside me. "How does your arm feel?" he asked.

"Fine, Coach," I said.

"Make sure you get some ice on it anyway, because

you're starting game two tomorrow," he said, keeping his voice low. "That okay with you?"

"You sure, Coach?" I said.

"Darnell," he said, "tomorrow you're gonna *make* me sure."

"Thanks," I said to Crockett. And silently, to Duke, Pee Wee, Joe, Campy and Jackie.

Chapter Twelve
The Fifth Night

We were almost at the villas when Joe Burgos showed up and pulled Coach Crockett aside. I could see him nodding as Burgos spoke. Then he shrugged and they both smiled. I wondered if they were talking about me, and I was proven right when Coach called me over.

"Darnell," he said, "there's been a little change in plans. I'll let Joe explain."

"It's not a big deal really, son," said Burgos. "I got a call from Charlie Sutton. He suggested that you might be more comfortable visiting with him at his house than here. He only lives a few miles away in Gifford, with his wife, who's a lovely lady. In fact, they've invited you to dinner as well. I checked with Coach here and he says it's fine. And since there's no evening run tonight, you'll be back in plenty of time for lights out. That is, if all this is okay with you."

I shrugged my shoulders. Truth be told, I was a little nervous about going to some old guy's house and leaving the team. But, if Crockett was okay with it, I couldn't really refuse; I mean, I was the one who'd instigated this whole thing. "That would be fine," I said.

"Great," said Joe. "Charlie said if you were on board with this, he'd pick you up in front of the registration building at 5 PM. I'll call him and tell him it's a go."

I went back to my villa and took a shower. Paco was suiting up for a visit to the pool, so I told him where I was going, and not to expect me till later.

"Have fun with the old folks!" he sang as he slung a towel over his shoulder and headed out the door.

* * *

At five o'clock on the dot a late model burgundy Cadillac that was buffed to a warm shine pulled up to the registration building, and the driver lowered his window. "Are you Darnell?" he asked.

"Yessir," I said.

"Well then, get in, son, I'm losing my air conditioning with this window down." He gave me a wink to show me he was just playing, but I was still a little nervous about the whole thing.

The car's interior, like the outside, was immaculate. The front bench seat was a buttery tan color, and I slid in next to Mr. Sutton and buckled up. He turned to me, and right away I could see that if he wanted to put someone on edge, he had the personality to do so. Charlie's skin was rather light but weathered, and his hair, which was mostly still there, was snow white. He kind of reminded me of the actor Morgan Freeman, though his voice was a lot higher and softer.

After we shook hands, he turned the Caddy around and we glided out of the main entrance. "How do you like the car?" he said, breaking the silence.

"It's real nice," I replied. "What year is it?"

"This, my boy, is a 1997 Cadillac Eldorado, which was a gift from the Dodgers for what they called 'fifty years of meritorious service,' though I stayed with them a lot more after that. I take a lot of pride in keeping it up."

"I can see that," I said. Charlie's car was a sweet ride, no doubt.

"'Course, me and the wife don't drive it much," he said. "Don't have many places to go, except grocery shopping, church, or stepping out for a bite to eat every so often. Sometimes we bring a picnic lunch to the public park at Vero Beach. They've got these covered pavilions where you can eat without getting fried by the sun. There is also a lounge nearby called *Bobby's* in the *Reef Ocean Resort* that's right near the boardwalk, where we go for lunch on a special occasion. It used to be *the* Dodger hangout for many years, till they up and left for Arizona. To me, the place has never been quite the same, but it does bring back memories. Happy memories, for the most part."

I nodded. "Why did the Dodgers leave Dodgertown, Mr. Sutton?" I asked.

"Long story. In the end, it was a combination of a couple things. You see, although Dodgertown was—and still is—the most famous Spring Training location, it didn't pay for the Dodgers to ship all their stuff way across the country from Los Angeles every year or to fly injured players back to the West Coast to see their team doctors. And then there was the fan base. Why would people who live near the beach in California want to come to Florida for the same thing? Dodgertown and Vero Beach was a vacation destination for the fans when they were based in Brooklyn, with its cramped city streets and cold winters. They considered it kind of a tropical paradise. But by the 2000s, the people who were fans of the Brooklyn club had started dying off. Look at me, son… I'm one of the last employees of the Brooklyn Dodgers to even be alive. I'm over eighty."

"You don't look it," I said.

"You're a bad liar," he replied with a chuckle.

"I'm surprised you don't live in Vero Beach," I said as we cruised away from Dodgertown.

"That's another long story. I'll tell it when we get to my house."

A few minutes later we entered the city limits of Gifford, which seemed situated a little north of Vero Beach, on US-1. There were signs for the town of Sebastian farther north. Charlie's house was on a nondescript street where all the houses looked the same: one-story bungalows with aluminum siding. Some had metal roofs and some had shingles. Some had an attached carport and a modest yard. Charlie's home stood out in that the lawn was extremely well-kept, as were the tropical shrubs out front. The windows facing the street all had flower boxes, too. And his mailbox was painted Dodger blue, with the team logo in white on one side and his house number on the other. We inched up the short driveway and came to a stop under the carport. Charlie turned off the motor.

"Gifford's a mostly Black community, Darnell," he said as the engine ticked down. "We've got some Latino families now, and a few whites, but it's still mostly colored. It was founded in the late 1800s by Black laborers who'd come to work on the Florida East Coast Railway. From there it kind of grew. But even so, we've got less than 10,000 people who live here. We're the in-between for Vero and Sebastian. Kind of the colored stepchild, and that was by design. Let's go inside."

I followed him in through the side entrance, where a

small white-haired woman, a little darker than him, was stirring a pot of something in the kitchen. "Mae, this is our guest, Darnell," Charlie announced a bit loudly; my guess was that she was a little hard of hearing.

The woman turned, wiped her hands on her apron, and came forward to shake my hand. "Pleased to meet you," she said with a distinctly Southern accent. "Charlie tells me you're a ballplayer from up north."

"Kansas City, Missouri, ma'am," I answered, and she nodded.

"Must be cold thereabouts right now," she said. "You must be happy down here in the tropics. And you're in luck, 'cause it's been a very mild spring."

"Yes, ma'am," I said. "It's been great."

"That's fine," she replied. "Well, I'll let you two men talk in the living room while I work on my collard greens. We're having them with chicken, and my special cornbread. Does that sound okay to you, Darnell?"

"It sounds fine, Mrs. Sutton," I said, though I'd never tasted collards in my life. My folks weren't much into Southern soul food.

Charlie reached into the refrigerator and pulled out a pitcher of lemonade, which he placed on the speckled Formica countertop while he fished a couple glasses from an overhead cabinet. The interior of the house, like the outside, was a bit worn, and the furniture and appliances a little outdated, but Charlie and Mae obviously took a lot of pride in what they had, though I got the feeling they didn't entertain too much.

Charlie motioned to me to follow him. I grabbed the lemonade pitcher and we went the few steps into his paneled living room. The only thing modern there was a bulky big-screen TV that rested on a low cabinet. Facing it was a black Naugahyde recliner and a reddish sectional couch, with lace doilies on the armrests. I set the pitcher down on Charlie's glass coffee table, but not before he'd placed a napkin under it. "Mae hates water rings," he said.

You're probably thinking the living room was a dreary old folks' kind of place, but that wasn't the case, because just about every wall was covered with neatly framed photos, both black-and-white and color, of the Dodgers during their tenure in Vero Beach. "Wow," I said, taking it all in. "This is really impressive, Mr. Sutton."

"Ah well, you know how it is, son," he replied with a dismissive wave. "You live a long time, you accumulate stuff."

"*I* don't think it's just stuff, sir," I said. "Do you mind if I walk around a little and see it all up close?"

"Be my guest," he said, settling into the recliner and pulling the handle to raise the foot support. "Just hand me a glass of lemonade first, would you?"

I gave him the drink and moved around the room, checking out the photos of Charlie as a young man during the Brooklyn years and seeing him age in images taken in recent times. The last one was of him sandwiched by Joe Torre, who managed the LA Dodgers during their last Spring Training at Dodgertown, and his coach Don Mattingly, who was now running the ballclub. Charlie was pictured with virtually every Dodger great from his half a century-plus with the team, from Jackie Robinson, Duke Snider, Pee Wee and Campy; through the '60s with Sandy Koufax, Maury Wills and Don Drysdale; to the '70s infield of Lopes, Cey, Russell and Garvey, and beyond. All the photos were autographed and probably worth a small fortune in total, but Charlie didn't seem too impressed. "Yeah, lots of years, lots of guys," he said as he sipped his lemonade.

I sat back down. "So, how did you come to be at Dodgertown in the first place?" I asked, wincing at the tartness of my drink, which had obviously been homemade.

"Ha!" he said, sensing my discomfort. "Mae doesn't make her lemonade too sweet, as you've noticed. That's the way we like it. But if you want me to get you some sugar—"

"No, this is fine," I assured him.

"Okay, then. So, to explain to you how I got to Dodgertown, I've got to go waaay back to 1945. Mr. Rickey—that's Branch Rickey, the man who signed Jackie Robinson—had bought into the club in '42. At the time I was a teenager living a couple blocks from Ebbets Field in Brooklyn in a rundown tenement apartment with my mother. My dad had been killed in combat somewhere in Europe in '44, and she had to raise me, her only child, pretty much alone. She worked two jobs, as a housecleaner and laundress, to keep clothes on my back and food on the table. And although she always stressed how she wanted me to go to college, I knew that I'd be done after high school. But meantime, I got a job during the baseball season on a crew that cleaned up Ebbets Field after ballgames. It was an okay job; I made a few bucks to put in the family till and got to see a lot of ballgames, though the Dodgers weren't into yet the team they'd become after Mr. Rickey signed Jackie.

"Anyway, my mom got cancer real bad, and it just ate her up. It was donations from our church that made it possible to give her a proper funeral. But I was now alone, with no clue what to do. So, one April day after the season started I went to the Dodgers' offices on Montague Street and presented myself at Mr. Rickey's door. When I told him who I was and that I was on the cleanup crew, he was a little taken back; but at the same time I think he admired the fact that I was willing to walk into his office and ask for a real job, because that's exactly why I was there.

"Now, understand that Mr. Rickey could be intimidating. He had this black hair and bushy eyebrows and a real gravelly voice. And, to tell the truth, he could be tight with a dollar. The sportswriters, and even some of the players, took shots at him behind his back. So, yes, he was a shrewd businessman and pretty… let's call it frugal. But he also had a sense of compassion. I told him my story, and I guess he saw something in me, the same way he did in Jackie. And so, beginning in 1946, I was hired on as an office assistant for the Brooklyn Dodgers. It didn't pay a lot, but I got to wear a shirt and tie every day, and that was better than a lot of colored men were doing back then. But, boy, they had me doing all kinds of things, from running errands to stuffing envelopes and the like. And once I got my driver's license, I made a lot of runs to LaGuardia Airport to pick up the Dodger executives or visitors from other clubs when they flew into New York. I worked hard and never took a day off, and it was noticed.

"So anyway, in '46 the Dodgers signed Jackie, and assigned him to our top minor league club in Montréal. As a colored man, this was a huge source of pride to me, though not everybody in the locker room was thrilled with having him there. At the time, the ballclub was spending Spring Training in Havana, Cuba, and some players actually tried to get a petition going to get him off the club. But the manager at the time, Leo Durocher, and

Mr. Rickey got wind of it and squashed the rebellion. I only heard about it through the grapevine, as I was back in Brooklyn helping get the office ready for when the club came north. As history will tell you, Jackie was not only a great success himself, but also opened the door for others to follow. And wouldn't you know it, the addition of Negro players put the Dodgers at the top of the National League for years to come.

"So now to Vero Beach. After the war, the big club had trained in Havana, like I said, and the Dominican Republic, while the minor league clubs—and there were a bunch of 'em —were in Pensacola, Florida. But for 1948, Mr. Rickey was looking for a Spring Training base in the States, one where he could house both white and Black players—hundreds altogether if you count the minor leaguers. I take it you've learned about segregation and the Civil Rights Movement and such in school?"

"Yessir," I said.

"All right, then, I'll keep going. So in '47 this man named Bud Holman, who was an executive with Eastern Airlines—which doesn't exist anymore—got the idea that his hometown of Vero Beach would be perfect for the Dodgers, because there was an available naval air station, with barracks facilities, which had been abandoned after the war and could accommodate a lot of ballplayers. Holman called Mr. Rickey and invited him down to take a look. So, Mr. Rickey and an assistant named Spencer Harris flew down, and did a preliminary scouting of the place. The club had had feelers from Daytona Beach, Sanford, Pensacola, and even a town in California, but they were leaning towards Vero Beach. Then, in November of '47, Mr. Rickey sent Buzzie Bavasi, another higher-up in the organization, down to take another look at Vero, as well as nearby Fort Pierce and Stuart. But Mr. Holman got ahold of Buzzie and wouldn't let go of him till he said yes to Vero. By December of '47, the deal was sealed. Now it was just a matter of converting the airbase to a baseball training facility.

"That's when I was told I'd be making the trip for that first spring, because I was needed there to assist Spencer Harris and Buzzie with getting the place up and running. I can't tell you how excited I was, son. Just the thought of leaving snowy, crowded Brooklyn for palm trees and sandy beaches had my heart racing. And even better, I'd be *flying* down with the front office staff! It gave me a lot of pride that they'd recognized my hard work and were rewarding me with this opportunity. What I *didn't* realize at the time was that I'd never see Brooklyn again."

"How come?"

"I'll get to that. So we got off the plane, and Mr. Holman and the mayor, a man by the name of Barber, were there to greet us. And while the surroundings were beautiful, with the palm trees and the tropical flowers and such, reality set in real quick. We had upwards of 500 players due to arrive in a couple months, and the place was a mess. So we rolled up our sleeves and got to work.

"First, we converted the officers' quarters—wood framed, two-story buildings on concrete blocks—into team offices, a dining room, and recreational facilities for players and staff. We scrounged furniture from other abandoned military facilities in the area. Meanwhile, the Ebbets Field groundskeeper, Eddie Durham, started carving out practice fields from the weed-infested lots behind the Quonset huts, where the players would be quartered. Little by little, the training facility took shape. Eventually, batting cages, practice mounds and the like were added. Then, one of the New York sportswriters gave it the name Dodgertown, which fit perfectly.

"That first spring was crazy. Players were everywhere—pitching, hitting, doing sliding drills. Mr. Rickey orchestrated the whole thing from a raised platform, deploying his baseball coaches. Some bleacher stands were erected near the fields so spectators could wander in and watch up close. It was like baseball heaven, at least to the casual observer. But to tell you the truth, the barracks, where the players slept six to a room, were pretty basic. There was no insulation, so they could get very cold at night and become sweatboxes during the day. We played a couple exhibition games on what's now one of the practice fields. The stadium, which would be named for Mr. Holman, wouldn't be opened until 1953."

"How did the players like it?" I asked.

"Well, like I said, it was pretty rough, and there were lots of rules, no matter if you were a low minor leaguer or on the big club. No smoking, drinking, or gambling in the barracks, with lights out at 11 PM. It was made clear to the players that we were guests of the city of Vero Beach, and we had to put our best foot forward." He paused, as if remembering something disconcerting. "To their credit, the Dodgers tried to provide pleasant diversions such as shuffleboard, croquet, pool tables, pinball machines, and movies in the evening. Later on, after Walter O'Malley bought out Mr. Rickey and took over ownership of the Dodgers, there would be tennis courts, a pool, a golf course, and even a man-made lake stocked with bass, so guys could go fishing. But let's face it, these were young men, many of them away from their homes and families for the first time.

So, while the players were not under orders to remain on the grounds, you couldn't fault them for wondering what was out there in Vero Beach. Truth is, there wasn't much: a few bars, a pool hall, a bowling alley, a roller-skating rink, and a lot of churches. It was Mr. Rickey's hope that the guys would stay close to the confines of Dodgertown, except to go to church on Sundays, but that wasn't always the case." Again, he paused a few seconds as if recalling something distasteful.

"Were there problems with the different races living together?" I asked.

"Oh, no," said Charlie. "Not if they wanted to stay in the organization, anyway. That was the whole idea of the place. Everybody got along just fine inside Dodgertown. It was safe and isolated from the reality of the South. You see, son, Vero Beach, like Florida and the whole South, was totally segregated. The Black players weren't welcomed at most places in town. And that applied to the wives of those guys on the big club whose families came down to visit. That's where I came in. You see, what few taxi cabs there were in town wouldn't even pick up colored people—neither would public buses. So, if Jackie's wife Rachel, say, wanted to have her hair done or do some shopping, I'd have to run her over to Gifford. Fact is, as nice as Dodgertown was, some of the Negro players—especially Jackie—felt confined. He even said to me one time it was like being on an Indian reservation. But the Black players didn't have much of a choice in those days. They just had to deal with it.

"Of course, things are different today, though it took a lot of time—*too much* time, if you ask me. Do you know that Holman Stadium had separate water fountains, restrooms, and seating in the beginning? Finally, Mr.

O'Malley's son Peter, who would take over running the team from his father, changed it all in 1962. Heck, the Vero Beach *public schools* didn't integrate until 1969, the year after Dr. King was assassinated." He shook his head and sighed.

"Could I ask you about some of the guys?" I said, wanting to change the subject without tipping my hand about my nightly adventures.

"Sure. I hope I remember. Let 'er rip."

"Duke Snider?"

"Ah, the Duke of Flatbush," he said with a smile. "Great player. He had all the tools, son. Duke sometimes got overlooked because there were two other great centerfielders in New York at the time named Mickey Mantle and Willie Mays. You've heard of them?"

"Sure," I said.

"But the Duke was right there with 'em. Could hit, field, and throw, yessir. Now, sometimes he could get down on himself, but that's where his teammates came in, especially the Captain."

"Pee Wee Reese?"

"Uh-huh. Now *there* was a leader. He was the glue to the club. Got along with everybody. Pee Wee refused to sign that petition against Jackie that I told you about, even though he was a Southerner. That showed me something. A good man, and a heckuva ballplayer."

"Joe Black?"

"Great pitcher—at least for one season, 1952. Then the coaching staff started tinkering with him, tried to get him to add another pitch or two, and he got all fouled up. He was gone a couple seasons later, to Cincinnati, and drifted out of baseball. A real shame."

"Robinson and Campanella?"

"Two great all-time players, but very different guys. Jackie was the ultimate competitor. He'd fight you to death, even if it was a game of checkers. But, oh Lord, he had a temper! You know, when Mr. Rickey signed Jackie, he made him promise not to have any outbursts for the first couple years, no matter what any opposing players did or said to him, and it got really bad at times. They called him names I can't even repeat, threw at his head, spiked him when he was turning a double play. But once Rickey lifted the restraints on Jackie, he gave it back *double*. The thing is, he could also be a little abrasive to his own teammates. Jackie was an agitator, especially in the civil rights area. If he felt the Negro players were being slighted in any way, shape or form, he piped up. Again, it was good to have somebody like Pee Wee to cool him down. But what a man."

Thinking back to the other night and my encounter with #42, I had to smile. You can read all the history books you want, but they don't begin to capture the fire that was inside that guy. Of course, I couldn't let on to Charlie that I'd seen it firsthand.

"Campy, on the other hand, wasn't a college man like Jackie, but he was like a coach on the field. He controlled that pitching staff and they listened to him, no matter what their color, because he knew what he was doing. Plus, the guy could hit a ton. But unlike Jackie, Roy was just so happy to be in the Major Leagues, living the good life as opposed to riding the buses all night and eating in greasy burger joints in the Negro Leagues, that he was hesitant to 'rock the boat' as they say. He absolutely loved Dodgertown, and even though his career ended tragically in a car accident in '57 that left him a quadriplegic, he never lost that optimistic disposition and continued to come down here for Spring Training for years afterward. I miss him. I miss *all* of them.

"You know, I was with the Dodgers in Vero from the beginning, through their transition to Los Angeles, and right up to the end. But those 1950s Brooklyn clubs were special. Not just because they were so danged good, but because of their makeup, their personalities. A group of very different men who came together for a common cause when it seemed the baseball world was against them… and showed us all what life could be like if we made the effort to live as one…" At that, a tear rolled down his cheek, and I felt bad because I'd maybe pushed him a little too far.

Fortunately, at that moment Mae called us in for dinner. Charlie slowly got up from the recliner—I now noticed that his six-foot frame was a little stooped—and led me to the kitchen.

Mae had outdone herself. A large serving bowl in the middle of the dinette table held the collards in a stew-like liquid to which a turkey leg and fragrant spices had been added; it was accompanied by a platter of fried chicken and a basket of cornbread, fresh from the oven. At each place setting stood a tall glass of sweet tea, condensation running down the sides.

"Wow," I said. "Mrs. Sutton, you didn't have to do all this."

"Hush," she replied. "I know the food at Dodgertown is probably very good, but everyone could use a home-cooked meal once in a while."

We sat down, and I was about to grab a hunk of cornbread when the Suttons reached out around the table. I took their hands and we all bowed our heads. "Lord," said Mae, "we thank you for your bounteous gifts and for our new friend Darnell. Please watch over him during his stay in Florida, and always. Amen."

After making sure it was now okay to eat, I dug in. Like I said, my folks aren't big on Southern food, but this stuff was off the chain. I kept telling myself not to pull a Paco and eat everything in sight.

We chatted about my high school, and what my favorite subjects were; then came baseball, and my ongoing efforts to help the team in the upcoming season. But when I felt we were getting too close to what was going on with me at night, I changed the subject. "So, how did you two meet?" I asked, figuring this would be a safe diversion.

"Well," said Charlie, "Mr. Rickey always said the only place he'd want to see his ballplayers outside of Dodgertown was at church. Of course, a lot of the boys didn't take him seriously, especially the ones on the big club. The married players had their families staying nearby and wanted to get out a bit. And the single guys, well, you know…

"But after a few springs on the staff, I figured that I should settle down, so I started attending church over here in Gifford. You see, Darnell, Negroes weren't welcome in the white churches in Vero Beach. I mean, there weren't signs posted or anything, but there was definitely that vibe, as they say today. So one Sunday in '53—this was after Mr. Rickey was bought out by Walter O'Malley, you understand—I was at service when I spied this lady here in the choir. Let me tell you, she was quite a songbird. And quite a dish, as well."

"Oh, stop," said Mae, giving her husband a gentle swat with her napkin.

"Anyway," he continued, "we eventually started

courting. Mae's family, the Bryants, had been in Gifford since the town got started, and they were suspicious at first of this stranger from Brooklyn, a place they'd only heard about in movies. But gradually, they got to like me, and we got married in '55, the year the Dodgers finally won a World Series for Brooklyn.

"By this time I was living at Dodgertown year-round. After the big club would go north and the many minor leaguers and their teams would scatter all over the country, I would help run the summer camp for boys that the Dodgers established, and during the fall I would take part in community events sponsored by the team. Now, I have to tell you, Mr. Rickey and Mr. O'Malley didn't like each a whole lot—in fact, after Mr. Rickey left, I always made it a point around Mr. O'Malley to not even bring Mr. Rickey's name up. But he, and later his son Peter who took over for him, always treated me great, and the O'Malleys put a lot of money into improvements in Dodgertown. I'd have to say it is what it is today because of the O'Malley family. Anyway, I was one of the few holdovers from the Rickey days.

"After Mae and I married, we decided to settle in Gifford. We just felt more comfortable here in the Black community. And though race relations in Vero Beach gradually improved and are pretty good today, we never felt the urge to move there. Mae wasn't able to have children, but she taught Sunday school at the church for years, and I became involved in community stuff, too. We've had a good life."

At this, Mrs. Sutton placed her hand on his and smiled, and it gave me a warm feeling. The meal had been terrific, and the Suttons couldn't have made me feel more welcome.

And then I went and ruined it.

"I'm wondering, Mr. Sutton," I said, sampling a piece of Mae's homemade pecan pie for dessert, "if you knew about what happened to my grandfather, Willie Jackson, when he tried out for the Dodgers?"

Everything immediately stopped. Husband and wife exchanged glances, but I couldn't read what those glances meant. So, I stupidly pressed on: "I mean, he was only here one spring, in 1953, but—"

"I knew your grandfather," Charlie said woodenly. "He was a good man."

"*Was*?" I said. "But he's still alive."

"He *what*?" they both cried.

"My grandfather lives with me and my folks," I said innocently.

"That can't be," argued Charlie. "His brother called after he'd left Dodgertown and said he was killed in a car accident."

"He never *had* a brother, Mr. Sutton," I whispered, wishing I'd never opened my mouth about my grandfather.

Again, the elderly couple shared a look. Then Charlie said, "Excuse us, Mae," and left for the living room. She just sat there with her head down. So, I followed Charlie out of the kitchen.

"Have a seat," he said, motioning me to the couch. He went to the cabinet under the TV and opened the bottom doors. Inside were binder-type scrapbooks, with various dates on their spines. He removed one labeled **1948-1953.** Then he sat next to me and laid the book on his lap. "I kept scrapbooks of all the years the club was in Dodgertown," he said. "This one covers the first few years. I guess you could call me the chief Dodgertown historian. I've been called upon to provide information to a lot of authors and such who were writing books about the Dodgers." He started leafing through yellowed newspaper articles, both from local papers and some up north, beginning with those announcing the Dodgers' move to Vero Beach. The book had been meticulously kept, as was everything else in Charlie's house.

As he slowly turned the pages, he said, "Like I told you, son, Dodgertown during Spring Training was filled chock-full of ballplayers, from the low minors to the big club. And even though it was hard to crack the lineup in the 50s because the team was so good, every ballplayer who came to Dodgertown during those years had a glimmer of hope. Your grandfather was one of those people."

He paused and stared at the wall, and then kept going on like he was in some kind of trance. "Willie Jackson came to us from the Kansas City Monarchs, where Jackie had gotten his start. He had a real live fastball, and a nickel curve that froze batters who were looking for the hard stuff. And he wasn't afraid to back people off the plate, no sir. Trouble was, he could be kinda wild with his control.

"We had this pitching contraption Mr. Rickey had devised called 'the strings.' Basically, it was these thin horizontal ropes made to look like a strike zone, and you had to place your pitches inside the strings. It's kind of like that wall they got there now with the square painted on it. That's where Willie ended up most days, and boy, did he hate it. But all our pitchers had to do it, even guys like Carl Erskine and Don Newcombe—"

"And Joe Black?"

"Uh-huh. In fact, it was Joe that really tried to help

Willie with his control, because the strings really frustrated him. But Willie could be a little, ah…"

"Headstrong?"

Charlie chuckled. "Yeah, you could call it that," he said. "But everyone could see his potential. Word was that he might be assigned to one of our AA clubs in Mobile or Fort Worth, or maybe even Montréal, which was our top farm team.

"Anyway, he was kind of up and down during camp that spring. One day he'd be striking out guys left and right, and the next he'd be walking the ballpark. But with a week to go, he was rounding into form and getting attention. In fact, some of the guys on the big club besides Joe noticed him and began working with him on the side. There were even whispers that he just might make it to Brooklyn as a relief pitcher if somebody went down with an injury."

"So… what happened?" I whispered, so nervous I was almost shaking.

"Well," he said with a sigh, "I told you that our colored ballplayers weren't welcome in Vero Beach. Do you know that one time the mayor, Barber, said he was afraid for the safety of the white girls in town because we had Negro ballplayers at Dodgertown? Anyway, the white players would go out here and there for a drink or two, and some of them would get into a little mischief, but we never had an issue. And the few Black players we had, as a rule, stayed in camp.

"But your grandfather, even though he was a young guy, had been with the Monarchs, and was used to touring the Midwest to other cities, and he got to feeling confined, the way Jackie did when he referred to Dodgertown as 'the reservation.' So, despite guys like Campy telling him to play it cool, he began to ask around about where he could go for some entertainment. Of course, all the guys told him Vero was a no-go, but that there was a place or two in Gifford where he could have a drink and relax a bit. Trouble was, nobody had cars, and the white taxis wouldn't take him there—"

"So he asked you."

Charlie nodded solemnly. "Yeah," he said. "He knew I drove some of the colored players and their wives here and there, and he started begging me to take him up to Gifford so he could unwind. Said the pressure to be successful was getting to him, and he had to blow off a little steam. So I finally broke down and said yes.

"It was the Saturday before we broke camp. The big club had already gone north and would be playing a string of exhibition games along the way. But a lot of the front office braintrust was still at Dodgertown, trying to decide who would be assigned to which minor league club and who would be released. And believe me, your grandfather was in the conversation for one of the higher clubs.

"I picked him up around 8 PM in the team car, which I really wasn't supposed to do, but I figured if I just got him away for a little while it would help him out. And I told him in no uncertain terms that we *had* to be back by the 11 PM curfew, or I was leaving him there. Of course he agreed, because he wanted to get out so bad.

"There were only two bars in Gifford, and I chose the better one, though they were pretty similar, to tell the truth. It was called *Smokey's,* and they had a live jazz band there on Saturday nights.

"Now understand, I wasn't courting Mae yet, and although I wasn't a night owl by any means, I used to take a drink now and then. And Willie was a year or so older and had been around. So, when we got there I tried to play host, show off a little, though I hardly knew anyone in the joint. They were all locals, and I was still really just an outsider. We had a couple drinks and talked about our goals and such—mine to have a career in the Dodgers' front office, while Willie wanted to pitch in the Majors. Then the band got going and the place started to fill up. I remember it was hot in there, and of course, in those days everybody was smoking, so there was this cloud of blue haze. But it was very mellow; Willie finally relaxed, and I was having fun as well. Maybe too much, because this young lady stopped by our table and started chatting, just being friendly, and of course we couldn't wait to tell her we were with the Dodgers over in Vero. Well sir, before you know it, here comes the girl's boyfriend, all lathered up because we were talking to his girl. He started getting loud, and stupid me, I stood up and started giving it right back, even though he was a good head taller. It was the liquor talking, you see.

"You two think you're hot stuff comin' in here, big baseball players tryin' to move in on our women!" he yelled, or something like that. So I said something back, and he hauled off and socked me. I went right down; then Willie jumped on him, and it became a Pier Six brawl in there. Old Smokey, who owned the place, went right to the phone and called the Vero Beach cops, who rarely ventured into Gifford, even though they were the only police force in the area. Fortunately, they showed up pretty quick and restored some kind of order, but not until the locals had blamed us for the whole melee. Smokey, who'd seen the whole thing and knew it wasn't really our fault, just suggested the cops get us out of Gifford, for our own safety if nothing else. And that they did—right to the

Vero Beach police headquarters, where they threw us in the drunk tank. And they weren't too nice about it, either.

"Well, they allowed us one call, and I had no choice but to call Dodgertown. Luckily, I got put through to Buzzie Bavasi, who was actually at a cocktail party Mr. and Mrs. O'Malley were throwing for some of the reporters before they left to follow the team north. He was furious, but agreed to come get us out.

"So we're sitting there amid the other drunks, and Willie had his head down. I asked him what was the matter and he said, "Charlie, in the fight somebody grabbed my arm and nearly tore it out of the socket. My right shoulder's on fire, man." His *throwing* shoulder. "I can't even lift my arm," he said, and there were tears in his eyes. I felt so horrible for him and apologized for drinking too much and acting like a fool, but he said it was his fault, that he'd dragged me out of Dodgertown in the first place. We were both miserable, waiting for Buzzie to pick us up.

"I was sure I was going to be fired and sent packing, so when Buzzie arrived, I begged him not to tell Mr. O'Malley and to give me another chance. I promised him I'd never take another drink the rest of my life. And I haven't. And Willie, bless him, backed me up and took all the blame on himself. Buzzie drove us back to Dodgertown, but he still hadn't made up his mind what to do with me. There was a story going around later that he'd called Jackie wherever the team was at that point and asked his opinion, and that even though Jackie acknowledged that what I had done was stupid, and that he and Campy and Joe Black would vouch for me and keep me on the straight and narrow whenever they were around. That must've carried a lot of weight. By the way, if Mr. O'Malley ever learned of the incident, he never let on.

"In the end, I got a stern reprimand but was allowed to keep my job. As for Willie, well, his arm was shot. I guess today you'd call it a torn rotator cuff, and back then there was no way to fix it. Besides, he'd now identified himself to the organization as a bad actor, and the Dodgers were very careful about negative behaviors in their colored players. So he was quietly released, and sent home on a Greyhound bus. Then, a couple months later I got that phone call from the man I thought was his brother, telling me he was dead. And that was that. Darnell, who do you think it was that called me?"

"My guess would be my grandfather himself, or maybe one of his friends. I guess he was so humiliated by the whole thing, he didn't want anybody to know, or even talk about it again. And he hasn't. Mr. Sutton, whenever the subject of the Dodgers comes up, the most he'll ever say is, "it didn't work out.""

Charlie shook his head. "He saved my job, saved my *life*, and I never got the chance to thank him," he moaned.

"Listen," I said, "I'll give you our phone number in Kansas City. Then, it's up to you if you want to reconnect with him."

"Do you think he'll talk to me?"

"There's only one way to find out," I said, and for the first time the old man smiled.

"Well, then, perhaps I have something for you as well," he said, and again began flipping through the scrapbook. He was near the end when he said, "Aha, here it is. I knew I remembered it." He carefully pried a brittle, yellowed photo from the page where it had been glued in. "Here's a picture of your grandpa from Dodgertown, spring of '53. Danged if you don't look a lot like him." He carefully handed it over.

"Thanks," I said, beginning to tear up myself. Then I just stared at the photo, and I've gotta tell you, it really shook me up.

Charlie drove me back to Dodgertown, and at first he didn't say much. I told him about our upcoming doubleheader with the Vero Beach High School the next day and invited him and Mrs. Sutton to come see it; he gave me a noncommittal nod. But when we rolled through the entrance, he said, "It gets so quiet and dark here at night. You know, even in those last years that I worked here, I could feel stuff in the air. I became really religious after that incident at *Smokey's*, you see. I figured God had better plans for me, but I had to shape up. So I did, and was fortunate to marry Mae. By the time all was said and done, I think I spent more time with the Dodger organization than anyone other than Vin Scully, their broadcaster, and maybe Tommy Lasorda. Anyway, religion-wise, I do believe there's such things as angels and spirits, and sometimes walking the grounds at night, I'd feel a… *presence,* you know? It was…"

"Magical?"

He nodded.

Chapter Thirteen
Game Day

I tossed and turned all night, replaying my conversation with Charlie Sutton over and over. While it was true that it cleared up a lot of stuff for me, it also presented new questions about my grandfather. And on top of that, I had to think about starting the second game today. I was lucky if I got three hours sleep and wished Coach Crockett would allow us to drink coffee with our breakfast, because I would've been chugging it.

As we were lying around before heading over the conference center, Paco broke down my performance the previous day. Even though he'd only faced me once—and got a hit, which he gloated over—Crockett had subbed in Babe for him the last two innings. But even so, he was watching me the whole time. "Bro," he said, "I don't know where you came up with that crazy windup, but you really had it working yesterday. You didn't tip what you are throwing at all, for one thing. And you were really hitting your spots. Frankie hardly had to work behind the plate. Whatever he called for, you put it right in there. I can't believe that just a few days ago you were throwing the ball all over the lot."

"What were the guys on your team saying?" I asked casually, though I was eager to hear the answer.

"Well, I can only go by what Kevin Bourke and the other starters were saying, not the subs… but they thought your stuff was absolutely *filthy*. And to be honest, I was lucky to get some wood on that curve you threw me and poke that dribbler up the middle."

"What about Trey?"

"Even the great Mr. Knight was impressed," he said, "though he'll never admit it. But then again, who cares what he thinks? He's all wrapped up in himself anyway. But I got to give the devil his due, he threw the ball good yesterday. Kept your team's hitters off balance for the most part. You probably had the most solid contact off him. He was also pretty ticked when you gunned him down at second, which was pretty funny. But anyway, if our team's gonna go anywhere this year, we need the both of you throwing good, so I can't be rooting against him."

"And Crockett?"

"You could see how pleased he was. He did mention to me between innings that you'll have to work on your pickoff move a little more with that big windup and all. And I'll have to be ready to come up throwing when there's men on, but it's nothing I can't handle. So overall, you really improved your status on the staff. And you're telling me you figured all this out yourself during the nighttime?"

"Yup," I said.

"Then maybe *you* should be coaching the team," he joked.

* * *

At breakfast (and, according to Paco, dinner the night before) the talk was about the previous day's game, and I got a lot of compliments at our table for my performance. Of course, Trey had to spit in the punchbowl when he questioned whether I'd be able hold runners on with my new delivery; Paco reassured him that we'd be working on it, and to just worry about himself. But overall, everybody was upbeat and looking forward to playing Vero Beach that afternoon. Crockett told us to eat our larger meal now and go light at lunch so the food wouldn't be sitting in our stomachs. And, of course, to hydrate. He also told us that he'd announce the lineups for the doubleheader at lunch, though I knew Trey and I would be the starting pitchers.

After breakfast I decided for the first time to check out the pool, which was really nice. It was hard to believe that the Dodgers had to put in their own pool, tennis courts, and eventually two golf courses, because Blacks were not allowed to use Vero Beach's back in the day. Anyway, although it was warm enough to swim, I was happy just to stretch out on a poolside recliner in a tee shirt and shorts and soak up the sun. It didn't take long for me to fall asleep, and I got back a couple hours that I'd lost the previous night. When I woke up it was nearly lunchtime, and I was refreshed and ready to go, despite the pregame butterflies that were beginning to swarm in my stomach.

As was his norm, Coach Crockett was jacked up before the doubleheader, and bounced all over the banquet area during lunch, checking in with pretty much everyone at one point or another; and Putney made sure all the pitchers weren't sore from the day before. Crockett told us that Amanda would be at the games and to report any soreness to her immediately so she could ice it up. Then it was time for the news everyone was waiting for: the starting lineups.

"Okay," he began, consulting his clipboard, "here's what Coach Putney and I came up with. Trey, you're starting the first game and you'll go the first four innings; Timmy Galvin will take the last three. Frankie, you'll open up at catcher, and Babe will finish it off."

"Not Paco?" interjected Trey, obviously disappointed that he hadn't drawn our best catcher as a battery mate.

"Nope," said Crockett. "I want him to sit out the first game because he caught the whole intrasquad yesterday, and besides, I need him to get some work with Darnell, who's starting game two."

"Okay," grumbled Trey, though he clearly wasn't happy.

The Crockett continued, "Both games we'll begin with Donnie at third, the Bourkes at short and second, and Igor at first. Tommy Lyons, Merc and Paul Chomicki in the outfield. Then I'll sub guys in. Like I said, Darnell's starting game two, with Sages relieving. Paco, if you start getting tired back there, I'll have Frankie or Babe spell you."

"*No problemo,* Coach," he said, shooting me a wink.

"Okay, then, go back to your rooms and suit up. We brought our road uniforms down because these games with Vero Beach have been in the works for weeks; you just didn't know about it. We'll walk to the stadium together and go through our normal pregame, but no BP. We had enough of that all week, and it's pretty warm out there. Are we good, gentlemen?"

We all nodded.

"Great. Then let's get after it."

* * *

I've always been pretty fussy about my uniform, and that day was no different. I made sure my royal blue jersey trimmed in white with *KC South* scripted across the chest was neatly tucked in, and I rolled my pants bottoms up and under to just below the calf, like I'd been directed. Then, I adjusted my blue hat with the interlocking white *KCS* logo till it sat perfectly on my head. I was checking myself out in the mirror when something struck me. When Coach Crockett had given us our numbers a few weeks back, the guys were allowed to make a request based on seniority, and many did (For example, Trey wanted #1, no surprise there). As for me, I was so screwed up at that point, not knowing if I was even going to play, that I told him I didn't care and would take anything. So, he reached into the jersey bag and pulled out #49.

Joe Black's number.

A coincidence? You tell me.

* * *

At the prescribed time we assembled outside the villas, in full uniform for the first time that spring, and it felt great (luckily, nobody ragged on me about my new-look pants). Most of the guys had their bat bags slung over their shoulders, and a couple of the sophs were recruited to lug the ball bags. When everyone was accounted for, Coach Crockett gave the signal, and we started walking as a unit along the cart path towards the footbridge. The practice diamonds were empty, which was strange, and there was a slight breeze that had the palm trees swishing. But the sun was strong, and I was glad I'd gulped a lot of water throughout the morning.

Of course, I had been the only one of us to cross the

footbridge already, and as our team gawked at the dense tropical foliage below, I thought back to the chill I'd gotten two nights back when the Dodgers' street clothes had morphed into uniforms. I wanted so much to scream out loud what I'd seen and experienced, but I realized it was something personal, something that would have to stay buried… for how long, I wasn't sure. But as I crossed the bridge again with my teammates, I felt a sense of pride that I had, for some reason, been chosen to experience those nights with the famous Boys of Summer.

As we were approaching Holman Stadium, the Vero Beach High School team bus pulled up, and the "Fightin' Indians" got off single file, dressed in their home white uniforms trimmed in red, with red caps and *VB* in white, outlined in light gray. They looked pretty sharp. From what I could see, their team appeared to be a fairly even mix of white, Black and Latino guys. Like us, they seemed to be excited about playing in such a cool place.

Once inside, the teams congregated on opposite sides of the field. Coach Crockett and Vero Beach's coach met at second base and shook hands, joined by Joe Burgos, who'd arranged the doubleheader. As they chatted, two umpires in full gear showed up and took a seat in one of the dugouts. Coach Putney circled us up for stretches and calisthenics on our side, and Vero Beach went into their pregame routine as well. Amanda Lisnow, assisted by a member of the grounds crew, set up a watercooler next to each team's bench, and some other workers started raking the infield, which looked pristine already.

Holman Stadium actually sat in a bowl, at least the playing field. From the box seats behind home plate, to the press box and the huge scoreboard in center field, it was Major-League all the way. Some puffy clouds scudded across the blue sky, and the Royal Palms beyond the outfield fence gently swayed. The place was picture-perfect, man.

Slowly, people started filing into the stands. I figured a lot of them were friends and family of the Vero Beach players; but there also seemed to be a bunch of senior citizens, who probably heard there was going to be a game at Holman Stadium and came out to pass a pleasant Saturday afternoon. There were also what appeared to be some families visiting on Spring Break from up north, as they seemed much more pale than the locals. Overall, it promised to be a decent crowd. Of course, a few of the guys started scoping the stands for cute girls, but I did my best to stay focused.

After stretching we broke up into pairs to get our arms loose, and then, with Putney's permission, I got a handful of guys together for a little Pepper, mostly those who missed out the previous day and wanted to get in on it.

Finally, Coach Crockett got us huddled. "Okay, gentlemen, we're gonna have the first base dugout," he said. "I talked to their coach, and for both games it'll be optional to use a designated hitter. So, we'll go with it in game one"—a decision, no doubt, based on Trey's pathetic batsmanship—"and our pitchers will hit in game two. I want you to understand that we're not here to play around, fellas. Vero Beach is a very good program, and as you can imagine, down here they play ball pretty much year-round. So it'll be a great test for us to measure ourselves against a quality team. Since we're the visitors we'll bat first in both games. Any questions?"

There were none.

"Okay then, bring it in tight." We came together and put in our hands. "Falcons on three. One, two, three—"

"*Falcons*!" we yelled in unison.

* * *

"Sit with me during the first game," Paco said to me. "We'll scout their team together."

"Deal."

Our hitters went quietly in the first inning, as their pitcher, a compact Latino lefty with good velocity, got ahead quickly and stayed around the strike zone. This wasn't going to be easy.

Meanwhile, Trey had his difficulties early on. Whether it was first-game jitters or whatever, he fell behind in the count and walked the first two guys he faced. Two hits followed, and we were down a couple runs before you could blink.

We managed to scratch out a run in our second at-bat, with Igor driving home Mercury, who'd stolen a base after patiently drawing a walk. Crockett, who was coaching third base while Putney coached first, clapped it up and kept up a continuous chatter of encouragement, as did the rest of us on the bench, but we seemed to be clearly overmatched.

"Okay, Bro," said Paco at the end of the second inning, "their hitters are good at working the count, but they're also crowding the plate and diving into pitches. We're gonna back 'em right out of there the first inning. Got it?"

"Got it," I said, encouraged that he felt my control had improved so much that I would be able to spot my pitches.

Trey settled down somewhat as the game progressed, but he never looked quite comfortable. Maybe he just didn't feel as confident with Frankie behind the plate, I don't know. But there was something else, and Paco caught it. After Vero Beach put across another run in the second inning, our ace stomped over to the edge of the bench, threw his glove down, and took a seat, where he proceeded to brood.

"Come with me," said Paco. I followed him to where Trey sat staring out at the field, and we plunked ourselves down on each side of him.

"What?" he snarled.

"Listen to me," said Paco calmly. "We're watching you, and you're tipping your pitches."

"No way," he snapped.

"Don't be a hammerhead," said Paco. "*Listen.* You're hesitating in your windup whenever you throw your curve. That's why they're sitting on your fastball. They know it's coming."

"Anything else?" Trey said sarcastically.

"As a matter of fact, there is. You're letting them get too comfortable in the box. Come up and in on 'em next inning."

I could tell that Trey was ticked at having me be privy to this conversation, so I just sat there impassively.

Predictably, Knight tried to place the blame on Frankie, trying to say he wasn't setting a good target, but Paco was having none of it. "Listen, Bro, I'm just telling you this before you hear it from Crockett and Putney. Next inning, take my advice and you'll be okay. I'll talk to Frankie and clue him in, too. *Comprendo*?" With that, he got up and sought out Lammers down the bench. Trey just continued staring out at the field, where Dirt Devil and Kevin Bourke were mounting a two-out rally in the top of the third.

At this point I fugured I'd put my two cents in. "Listen, man," I said. "If we're gonna be any good this year, you and I gotta lead the way. So listen to Paco. He knows what he's talking about. And when I pitch later on, I want you to keep an eye on me, too. That's the only way we're gonna get better, Trey." I gave him a pat on the shoulder (instead of a smack upside the head, which is what he really needed) and left him alone.

Now, I wish I could tell you that my little heart-to-heart with Mr. Wonderful got him on the right track, but he *was* a real hammerhead. He went right back out there and continued what he'd been doing. And Vero Beach, to their credit, kept hitting rockets off him. If it wasn't for our guys, particularly Dirt Devil and the Bourkes, making diving stops to prevent more guys from scoring—after he'd walked them, of course—we would've been down by more than six runs when his four-inning stint was over. And when Coach Crockett pulled him aside and tried to talk to him on the bench, I could see he was *still* maintaining it wasn't his fault.

So, Galvin pitched the last three innings, as did Vero's relief pitcher, and we managed to get a few runs back while only surrendering one more in the meantime. But they were good team, man, well coached on the fundamentals. They hit-and-ran, stole bases, and always hit the cutoff on outfield throws. Like I said, only great fielding plays on our part, along with some timely hitting, kept it respectable.

Before the game was even over, Paco tapped me on the shoulder. "Let's go warm up in the bullpen," he said. "I've seen enough." We walked down the right field line to where the bullpens were located, in a fenced off area adjacent to the right field corner. "Wow, some cute babes here today," observed my catcher as we strolled along. Then he said, "Yo, Bro, someone's waving at us." I looked up and saw Charlie and Mae. Both had these big Panama hats on. Charlie gave me a thumbs-up, and I returned it, determined not to let him down.

Between games our coaches gathered us together. "Okay, gentlemen, that wasn't too pretty," said Crockett. "Just understand that they've been practicing a whole lot longer than us. Still, there's no excuse for us not to play better in this game coming up. You've gotten all the first-day nervousness out of your system, so let's just flush that game and get after 'em. Darnell, you ready to go?"

"Yessir," I said.

"All right then," he said. "Let's give Dodgertown a proper sendoff." We put our hands in and did our Falcons chant.

Again, we were up first, and Crockett had inserted me into the three hole in the batting order. Vero Beach had a big blond right-hander going, a real surfer dude type. He struck out Mercury on a nasty curve, but then Kevin Bourke singled to left. As I was digging in at the plate, I spied Kevin creeping off first base out of the corner of my eye. I knew I had to do my job here to advance the runner, so I choked up a little on the bat handle and tried to find something I could work with. Vero's pitcher got ahead of me 0-2, but then he tried to waste one outside and I stroked it just inside the right field line. By the time their fielder dug it out of the corner, I'd cut the bag and was gliding towards second. My pop-up slide beat the throw by a mile, and Bourke scored to put us ahead. I called time and dusted myself off; and as I looked up, I could see five guys sitting by themselves on the distant grassy berm beyond the outfield fence, under the Royal Palms. They were all applauding. I couldn't make out their faces, but I was pretty sure that three of them were dark and two were not.

We ended up scoring another run before our half inning was over, and I took the mound ready to rock. And though I really wanted to look back at those guys on the berm, and Charlie, I knew it was time to focus. I took my warmup throws, and then Paco rifled the ball to second and the guys threw it around the infield. Igor, the last guy to handle the ball, walked it over to me and placed it in my glove. "You're the man, Darnell," he said, and jogged back to first.

Then, deciding not to change the ritual that had worked the previous day, I again grabbed the peace sign around my neck, touched it to my lips, tucked it inside my undershirt, and whispered to myself, "Pressure is a privilege." It just felt right, and that's why I've done it ever since.

As I rubbed up the ball, I took a deep breath and drank it all in as I tried to calm my breathing. It had been a crazy week from beginning to end, and it had all come to this. But as jacked as I was, I couldn't help feeling that this had all been preordained, that I was *meant* to be here in Dodgertown on a balmy spring day, on the same mound where Joe Black and so many other greats had pitched over the years. It was like I was part of some kind of continuum, and I was being called upon to play my role.

So, what did I do? I walked the first batter, of course. Like I said, the Vero Beach guys were disciplined at the plate, and though I wasn't missing by much, they knew enough to lay off. So the guy walked on a 3-2 pitch, and as he jogged to first, Paco stepped out in front of the plate and fired the ball to me. "Hey Bro, relax," he said with a wink. "It's all good."

Now I had a problem. With a man on, I had to modify my full windup and go back to something like what Coach Putney had made me switch to last season. Sensing the baserunner might try to steal, Paco called for a fastball. I nodded, rocked, and dealt a strike, which the batter swung through. In the background I could hear Igor yell, "He's going!" and immediately bent over as Paco came out of his crouch like a panther and gunned down the runner with room to spare.

"See what I mean?" Paco said to me as the retired runner jogged back to the Vero Beach dugout. "Now let's get to work."

Which is exactly what I did. Remembering Paco's instructions about Vero Beach crowding the plate—and Jackie Robinson's declaration that I *owned* the plate—I constantly backed them out. That, combined with my windmill delivery, had them totally befuddled, swinging at air. In the second inning, one guy tried to challenge my elaborate routine by laying down a bunt, but Joe's delivery had taught me to end up totally balanced, and I easily fielded the ball and threw him out. With every successive out our bench got louder and louder, and when I would leave the field after the third out of each frame, I could hear the Holman Stadium crowd applauding me, too. Even Trey managed a sheepish "Nice inning" a couple times.

Meanwhile, feeding off my success, our hitters came to life, pounding the surfer dude and the two Vero pitchers who followed him. By the fourth inning I was 3-

for-3, with two doubles and a single. Not bad for a starting pitcher. And Paco actually lifted one over the left field fence for a Major League-distance homer.

Originally, I'd figured I was only going to pitch the first four frames, but when I got to the bench Putney asked if I thought I might have another inning in me. "Sure," I said, and proceeded to strike out the side on ten pitches.

The game ended as a 9-2 blowout, and Coach Crockett was really happy. We lined up for high fives with Vero Beach, and a lot of them had good things to say to me like, "You were tough today, man," and "Great stuff, I couldn't catch up to you." After that was over, we came together, and Crockett set us down on the outfield grass. "Now that's more like it," he said proudly, with Putney nodding behind him. "You showed those guys what KC South baseball is all about!"

We set up a cheer.

"Boys, we had a great week down here," he continued. "You worked your butts off all week, behaved like gentlemen, and left a good impression on the folks at Dodgertown. I have to tell ya, it wasn't easy putting this trip together, and a few things had to break our way to make it happen, but the effort was well worth it. Coach Putney and I couldn't be prouder of you."

We cheered and high-fived each other again.

Then Crockett raised his hands and quieted us down. He said, "And now, as a reward for all your efforts this week and the way you carried yourselves down here, we have a little surprise in store for you. There was a little money left in the kitty because we didn't do anything all week but eat, sleep, and play ball. But tonight's our last night before we fly home tomorrow, and Mr. Burgos helped us get a dinner reservation this evening at a nice seafood place on the beach. So, we'll go for our team meal there, and then maybe check out Vero Beach. Just no swimming, okay?"

Another cheer.

"Dress code is casual but neat, fellas. No sweatpants or hats inside the restaurant. We're gonna look like a first-class program, as always."

Igor put his hand up. "Can we take off our sneakers on the beach, Coach?" he asked, drawing raucous laughter.

"Yes, Igor," he replied patiently. "Just stay out of the water." He looked at his watch. "Okay, it's half-past four," he said. "Go back and shower and make yourselves presentable. The bus will leave from outside the villas at six."

We got up to go, but I wasn't done. First, Amanda came over to check on me. "How's that shoulder?" she asked, arching an eyebrow. "Are we feeling better?"

"Yeah, no problem," I said, a little embarrassed.

"A dose of confidence will do that," she replied. "Good luck this season."

Right behind her were Charlie and Mae, and both of them were beaming as if I were their own grandson or something. "Tremendous outing, Darnell," said the old man. "You had those Vero Beach boys off balance all day."

"And you can hit, too!" added Mae.

"Thanks," I said. "I appreciate you coming out on this hot day."

"We're used to it," said Charlie. "You know, I haven't been to a ballgame in a while. It was an enjoyable afternoon."

"When are you going home?" asked his wife.

"Tomorrow morning we're busing back down to West Palm Airport," I said. "But tonight, the coaches have arranged for us check out the beach and have dinner."

"How nice," said Mae. "Well, enjoy yourself, and good luck back in Kansas City."

"Thanks," I said. Then I turned to Charlie. "Mr. Sutton," I said, "I really appreciate you and Mrs. Sutton welcoming me into your home and telling me all about Dodgertown and my grandfather. I hope the two of you reconnect in the future."

"Well, we'll see," said Charlie, leaning on his cane. "But I have to say, when you were out there I could've sworn I was watching Willie Jackson. I'll be following your career, son, so don't disappoint me!"

"I won't." And I gave them both a both a big hug.

* * *

That evening we rode the bus through the town of Vero Beach to the bridge that took us over the Indian River Inlet to the stretch of beach along the famous A1A Highway, which runs the length of Florida along its eastern coast. It was another gorgeous evening, and palm tree-lined streets gave way to chic restaurants and high-rise resorts that looked out over the water. We ate at a cool place called *Mulligan's*, which was really laid-back and decorated in a tropical motif. The waitstaff pushed three long tables together for us and served us all kinds of seafood and salads, which we ate family-style, washed down with countless pitchers of iced tea. All the other patrons of the place, which was packed because of Spring

Break, looked at us like we were some kind of celebrities, which we didn't mind, especially those of us—including me—who were checking out the beautifully tanned girls that seemed to be everywhere.

Finally, towards the end of dinner, Coach Crockett stood up and raised his glass of tea in a toast. "To Dodgertown, and a great season for the KC North Falcons!" he said.

"Hear, hear!" piped in Putney.

After dinner our group of very stuffed ballplayers wandered down to the beach and took off our shoes for a surfside stroll. The sand was cool between my toes, and a steady breeze came off the frothy waves that crashed on the shore. Seagulls swooped overhead in the early evening sunset. Behind us, people young and old strolled on the boardwalk, which ran the length of the public beach.

"You pitched lights out," said Paco as we walked along the shore, stopping to scoop up a souvenir seashell here and there. "Don't be surprised if you're now the number one starter on the staff."

"You think so?" I said.

"Oh yeah. I heard Crockett and Putney talking back at the villas," he said. "If you keep looking like you did today, you'll be our ace. You watch." We took a seat on the sand and listened to the sound of the ocean. "Someday I'm gonna move near the beach," he said. "I'm tired of cold winters and blazing hot summers with no ocean to go to. This is the life, Bro."

"You got that right."

And then something happened. Trey Knight shuffled over and sat himself down next to us. For a few moments it was quiet and awkward. And then he said,

"You guys were right today. Paco, I should've pushed Vero Beach's hitters off the plate. But I'm worried about tipping my pitches. Crockett and Putney picked up on it, too."

"I knew they would. But don't worry, Bro, we'll work on it," said Paco, trying to play it cool.

"And Darnell, what you told me, about our team's chances this season and all, made a lot of sense. I'm, uh, sorry for breaking your stones so much. You threw the ball great today."

"Thanks," I said. "I've got a good feeling about this season, like I told you. But we're gonna need you, Trey."

"No doubt," chimed in Paco. "Just be glad you two have an all-conference catcher to keep you in line."

* * *

That night I slipped out of our villa for the last time. It was kind of cloudy and breezy, but I couldn't leave Dodgertown without taking one last spin around the complex. Of course, a part of me was wondering if Duke, Pee Wee, or any of the others would be waiting for me at the footbridge… but it was empty. Even so, I stayed there a long time, leaning on the metal railing and staring off into the underbrush, replaying in my mind everything from this remarkable week. And I wondered again if it had all been a dream. But then, I knew better.

It had all really happened.

And it was magical.

Chapter Fourteen
July, 2021

Rosa Santos and Darnell Hayward sat quietly, sipping their coffee in the corner booth of a café near Dodger Stadium, where the home team would play the Arizona Diamondbacks that afternoon, the last game before the All-Star break. Their record stood at 56-34, good enough for second place in the National League's Western Division. The San Francisco Giants, to everyone's surprise, had jumped out to an early lead in the standings and maintained a slim two-game lead over the Dodgers.

For his part, Darnell had fit nicely into the Dodger bullpen, pitching mostly in middle relief and posting a very respectable ERA of 2.78 in 25 appearances. As he had promised manager Dave Roberts, Hayward happily accepted whatever task he was presented with and gave the club a solid effort. Of course, middle relievers in the Major Leagues are mostly unsung heroes, the guys who bridge the gap between a ballclub's high-priced starters and their closer. And the Dodgers, with pitching stars such as Clayton Kershaw and Walker Buehler, had a strong staff from top to bottom.

Unfortunately, a big-time free agent pitcher, who had come to the club in the off-season with much more fanfare than Darnell, was the source of yet another media firestorm—and another black eye for Major League Baseball—when he was suspended for behavioral misconduct relating to women, a story that Rosa was all too familiar with. It was no wonder that she covered this ongoing affair with a jaundiced eye, and again questioned both her career path and her involvement in the game.

As she slowly stirred more sugar into her cup, Darnell watched her closely. "Feel like talking?" he asked.

"I'm sorry," she replied. "With the suspension story and all, I've been a little distracted. I'm glad the All-Star break is coming up. I really need some time away."

"Uh-huh. Well, would you care to, uh, talk about *my* story? That's why we're here, after all."

"I know." She looked upwards, as if trying to find words. Then she fixed her eyes on his and said, "It's a fine story, Darnell, but I just don't know if I buy it."

"Really?"

"Really. I mean, you're very convincing, and I totally think *you* believe it, but come on. Ghosts running around a ballfield? Giving you midnight baseball lessons? It's a bit much."

He leaned in and whispered, "Maybe you just need something to believe *in*, Rosa."

"Maybe. But I'm a journalist, Darnell. I deal in facts, many of them double and triple-checked. There is no way to quantify everything you've told me. None of your coaches or teammates knew what was going on with you in 2012. It's all just hearsay. How do I know you wouldn't have developed into a fine pitcher on your own?"

"You don't."

"Precisely. That's why I can't buy in. Listen, like I said, you're a nice guy with what I think are the best of intentions, but I think you've picked the wrong person to pitch this to."

"No, Rosa," he said, "you're wrong. In fact, you're *exactly* the right person to share this with. I told you that way back, the first time we ever talked. Remember?"

"Yes."

"The thing is, if you thought I was just BS'ing you all along, why have you put in so much time meeting with me and all? You could have cut me off at any time."

"That's true," she said, and signaled the waitress to top off her coffee.

"So why have you hung with it? There's gotta be *some* reason."

"I honestly don't know," she confessed as the waitress hurriedly poured and moved on.

Hayward took a deep breath and gave the tabletop a few taps. "What if I told you I could prove to you that what happened to me isn't a fairytale?" he asked.

"Prove it? How?"

"Let's just suppose I knew how to do it. Would you be willing to play along?"

"Depends. What do you have in mind?"

"Okay, hear me out, and don't say anything until you think it over. A couple days ago Skip pulled me aside and told me that down in Vero Beach they're opening a new indoor facility at Dodgertown—only it's not Dodgertown, or even Historic Dodgertown, anymore. A year or so ago MLB took it over and renamed it the Jackie Robinson Training Complex. They poured a lot of money into improving and modernizing the facilities, apparently, and this week during the All-Star break they're dedicating this huge indoor building which will have batting cages, weight rooms, and a ton of other stuff for teams—both men and women—to come train there. And even though the complex isn't specifically tied to the Dodgers anymore, the Commissioner called us and wondered if we would like to send a representative to the opening ceremony. So, Dave Roberts made the announcement to the team the other day and asked if anyone was interested.

"Well, you know how it is. Unless guys are actually playing in the All-Star Game, the last thing they want to do is something regarding baseball. Most of my teammates are either flying home to spend time with their families or have planned vacations. So there were no takers, which is understandable. But the more I thought about it, the more I was convinced it was something I needed to do."

"How come?"

"I don't know, maybe it's a closure thing. Anyway, I would only have been hanging around in Kansas City anyway, because my wife is tied up with family business and stuff. And besides, it would only be for a couple days. So, I approached Skip and told him I'd do it. He was happy, because when he'd played for the Dodgers in the early 2000s, he'd gone to Spring Training at Dodgertown and has fond memories of the place. But of course, he's managing the National League All-Star Team because we won the championship last year. When I told him I had actually gone down there when I was in high school, he said I'd be the *best* guy we could send."

"Sounds like a great trip down memory lane for you," she said, a hint of sarcasm in her voice.

"Yeah, maybe," he replied. "The Dodgers are flying me down there, charter, tomorrow morning." He paused and stared at her hard. "I think you should come along for the ride."

"*Me?*"

"Yes, you."

"Why?"

"I can't put it into words exactly. But I feel that if you just go there and *see* the place, everything I've told you for the past few months will make sense. Unless you've got other plans for the All-Star break, that is."

"No, no plans," she said. "Except maybe cleaning out my refrigerator. But still, I really need a break—"

He raised his hands and said, "I totally get it if you don't want to do it. Do me this favor. Think about it during the game today and tell me your answer afterwards. Either way, I'll be okay with it. Deal?"

She frowned and slowly shook her head… and then she said, "Deal."

After a 22-run barrage the previous day, the Dodgers kept things going with a 7-4 victory behind starter Tony Gonsolin, powered by a homer from All-Star Mookie Betts and clutch hits from Justin Turner and Chris Taylor. Darnell was not called upon to pitch this day, so he spent a pleasant afternoon in the bullpen discussing plans for the break with his fellow relievers.

Meanwhile, Rosa took notes in her press box perch for the *El Comentario* story she'd have to file at the end of the game. Still, the writer couldn't help thinking of Darnell's offer earlier that day. Everything in her rational mind told her this was not a good idea. First, she'd be traveling in the company of a handsome ballplayer who also happened to be married, though from what she'd observed so far this season, he was nowhere near the typical party animal type she encountered among Major Leaguers. And after what had happened to her the previous season and the stigma that had attached itself to her as a result, she was hardly in a position to have a reason for people to suspect her of conduct unbecoming of a journalist.

In addition, she was badly in need of a rest. The first half of the season had been a grind, despite the Dodgers' success so far. Dave Roberts had them playing good ball, and a close pennant race with their longtime nemesis San Francisco Giants added a lot of spice to the season. But this was counterbalanced with the new off-the-field scandal that she'd been forced to cover, one that only served to reinforce her lack of faith in the game.

But even more important was the fact that although Darnell was a normal enough guy, his story was *way* out there, to say the least. The thing was, he seemed to believe it so fervently, and was so specific in its telling, that she had looked forward to their top-secret meetings, making sure to either write down notes upon her return home or to whatever hotel she was staying at during road trips, or dictate a critical commentary into her palm-sized tape recorder once their session had ended. She had also taken the time to read up on the history of Dodgertown, and of the 1953 Brooklyn ballclub, to see if he had erred in any of his facts. They all checked out. She even looked up Willie Jackson, the grandfather, and saw that even though Negro League records could sometimes be spotty, he did indeed spend three seasons with the Monarchs, compiling a solid won/loss record, which could logically have led to a tryout with Brooklyn in Dodgertown. But still… ghosts giving a high school kid pitching lessons at midnight? It couldn't be true.

But what if it *was*?

* * *

After the game Darnell stayed at his locker for a while, though he'd played no role in today's contest. Instead, those reporters who did come over asked about his plans for the break. When he told them where he was going, and why, they didn't seem too impressed. "Oh, that's nice," was the typical answer, or something along those lines. Dave Roberts thanked him again for volunteering to represent the team, and Scott Akasaki, the Dodgers' traveling secretary, told him a small jet chartered by the club would be waiting for him at LAX at 6 AM the next morning, which meant he wouldn't be getting into the small Vero Beach Airport until about 1:30 PM Eastern time. Then, he would have the option to fly home the same day or stay over in Vero Beach, where he had been booked a single room in a luxury hotel near the beach.

"Could you reserve a second single?" he asked. "I might be taking a friend with me."

"I could upgrade you to a double," Akasaki suggested.

Hayward chuckled. "No, that won't be necessary. And I'm not even sure the person's coming."

"No problem," Scott said, jotting down the memo. "You can always cancel it if the person doesn't make it."

Darnell wolfed a sandwich from the team buffet, finished dressing, and left the locker room, heading for the players' parking lot, where he'd get into his leased BMW and return to the apartment he was renting in the suburbs of LA. He'd already told his wife that he wouldn't be coming home for the All-Star break, which was a disappointment of sorts; however, he knew Tami and Jacqui would soon be coming to spend the summer with him now that school had let out for the year. He also planned on flying his parents out there for a week; hopefully, they'd be able to make it.

Once outside, Hayward signed a few autographs for what seemed like the same fans who stalked the players every day they played at home, making sure to keep moving towards the car. But as he approached the vehicle, he was surprised to see Rosa Santos leaning against the front bumper. "Nice wheels," she said. "Hope I'm not scratching the paint."

"No big deal," he replied. "Besides, it's a rental."

"I figured."

"So, did you wait all this time to talk about my car?"

"Nope," she said. "I came to tell you I'll be going to Dodgertown with you."

"You mean the Jackie Robinson Training Complex," he corrected, smiling wryly.

"Whatever. And how will we get there?"

"Simple. Meet me at the Departures entrance at LAX a little before 6 AM. The Dodgers are flying us down there on a business jet to Vero Beach Airport, which is small, but big enough to accommodate that kind of plane."

"Sounds good. And we're coming home the same day?"

"Depends on how the day goes. If we want to stay over, they've made accommodations for us. Separate, of course."

"Of course."

"You need a ride to the airport tomorrow?"

"No, I can get there myself," she assured. "I just hope this will be worth my while."

"It will be, Rosa," he said. "Trust me."

Chapter Fifteen
Vero Beach

When the taxi transporting Rosa to the airport pulled up to the Departures entrance, Darnell was waiting, a Dodgers travel bag slung over his shoulder. He was dressed in a light blue suit with an open neck dress shirt, nothing too formal. She had chosen a simple cotton dress and Espadrilles, and likewise had come prepared with an overnight carry-on, which she pulled along. In her other hand was a huge travel mug of coffee.

"Glad you made it," he said, taking her bag. "Let's go find our plane."

They were directed to a special gate where they were escorted to a sleek corporate jet that sat waiting on the tarmac. Besides the pilot and a small crew, they would be the only occupants.

"Fancy," observed Rosa as they climbed aboard.

"One of the perks of being a Major Leaguer," he explained with a smile.

The cabin was small but comfy, and they buckled into their seats, which were separated by the aisle. A male attendant stopped by to tell them they would be served breakfast once they were airborne, and that their flight time would be a little over four hours.

"Do you mind?" asked Rosa, producing her ever-ready tape recorder. "There's a few loose ends to this story I want to get cleared up."

"Why not?" he answered. "We've got four hours. Ask away."

"How did your senior season go?" she began as the plane started to taxi down the runway.

"Well, because of that week down in Florida we had a real advantage over the other teams in our conference, so we got off to a flying start. As a courtesy to Trey, Coach Crockett started him in our first game, and he pitched pretty well overall, but by mid-season I was the ace. With our lefties Galvin and Sages spot-starting to give us some rest, we cruised through the regular season with only two losses, then won the championship game, where I tossed a three-hit shutout. My whole family was in the stands, including my grandfather, which was very cool."

"What happened to the other guys on the team?"

"Really, the only guys who got scouted were me, Paco and Trey, and the interest in him was based mostly on what he'd done his junior year. Some of the guys ended up playing D-3 or D-2 ball. Paco got signed by the Padres right out of high school, but he never got out of single-A ball. Last time we talked, he was playing in the Mexican League and enjoying the beach there."

"And Trey?"

"Well, Trey being Trey, he refused to 'waste time' in college as he put it, got signed to a minor league deal with the Cardinals, and blew his elbow out in rookie league ball, probably trying to impress people by throwing too hard. I have no idea where he is now."

"What about your coaches? They played a major role in all this, right?"

"No doubt. I mean, even though their efforts to help me didn't pan out, they never stopped trying, never gave up on me, and I owe them a lot of gratitude.

"Coach Crockett stayed a few more years at South, then joined the baseball staff at the University of Missouri. He's since retired and runs a baseball training center for high school players in Arizona. And Coach Putney, although he doesn't do baseball anymore, is still teaching physics at South. To this day he calls me his 'greatest experiment,' and won't let me forget how I almost killed him down in Florida."

"So you're the only one who made it to The Show."

"Yeah, but like with anyone else, it was a mixture hard work, luck, and timing.

"My parents were adamant about me going to college, so we had a deal: I would attend Iowa Western Junior College, which is one of the best baseball programs in the Midwest—and fairly close to home—and see if I got drafted from there. If not, I'd hopefully get a scholarship to a big school, maybe Mississippi State or LSU or one of those southern teams, so I could play in warm weather and finish out my degree."

"In what?"

"Don't laugh, but psychology. I guess I wanted to figure out what made me such a head case in high school."

Breakfast arrived, a full tray that included eggs, bacon, hash browns, cereal, and toast, with a fresh pot of coffee. They both dug in and continued to talk.

"Junior college was okay," said Darnell as he buttered his toast, "though Iowa isn't exactly a hopping place. Maybe that was just as well, though, because it made me concentrate on baseball and my studies.

Overall, I ran a 3.5 GPA, which I was proud of, because a lot of guys were just there to play ball and hardly went to class. Of course, once again, I was one of the few Black guys in the program, but it all worked out. I had good coaching, and they didn't try to make me change my delivery, not that I would have anyway. I was staying with Joe Black's method, no matter what."

"Okay," she said, though he could sense that she still wasn't on board with the Dodgertown ghost story. "And from there?"

"Well, since it was the Midwest, the Royals had a scout in Iowa Western's territory. I put in two solid seasons there and our team won a lot of games, so I got noticed. The Cardinals were interested, too, but I couldn't say no to my hometown team when they offered me a modest bonus to sign.

"So, long story short, I moved up the Royals' minor league ladder pretty quickly, from Lexington to Northwest Arkansas to Omaha. Unfortunately, while I was in the minors I missed out on the Royals winning the World Series in 2015. The good thing is, by midseason of 2018 with Omaha, the Royals were rebuilding and had some injuries and needed some arms in the bullpen. I'd been converted to a reliever in the minors, mostly because I was a two-pitch pitcher, so I fit right in when they called me up. Again, it was a real big deal during my first homestand at Kaufman Stadium. Not only my family, but a lot of my old teammates and coaches came out to support me. And that first game Ned Yost, our manager, threw me in for some middle-inning relief and I pitched two scoreless frames, only allowing one hit without giving up a run.

"You know the rest. When my contract ran out this

year and I became a free agent, there was only one place I wanted to go: to the Dodgers. It was something I felt I had to do to come full circle."

Rosa turned off the tape recorder and slipped it into her carry bag. They had been talking for over an hour, and the large breakfast and early departure this morning had left her sleepy. "Mind if I catch a few winks?" she said, shifting her plush seat into full recline.

"Not at all. I didn't sleep much last night myself. Too excited about today. We've got a long day ahead of us down there, so we might as well rest up."

Within minutes they were both out cold.

* * *

Both Darnell and Rosa awoke shortly before their chartered jet touched down in Vero Beach. This gave them time to freshen up in the surprisingly spacious restrooms on board. They stepped onto the hot tarmac on a sweltering July afternoon, the heat radiating up through the soles of their shoes. Fortunately, after retrieving their bags they didn't have to wait long, as a blue SUV was close by, its female driver waving them over. "Hi!" said the young lady while taking their bags and stowing them in the back of the car. "I'm Brandi Hackett, the Marketing and Retail Coordinator here at the complex. I've been deputized by our Managing Director, Rhonda Madeiros, to come get you. I hope you had a good flight from Los Angeles. You must be tired."

"No, we're fine," said Darnell as they hopped into the air-conditioned SUV. "We had breakfast and a few hours' sleep on the way over, and we're raring to go." Then he formally introduced himself and Rosa, whom he called "the Dodgers' beat reporter for one of the most respected Hispanic newspapers in the country," which left the journalist blushing.

"That's impressive," said Brandi. "It's great to see a woman in such an important position." If she knew anything about Rosa's notoriety over the past year's tribulations, she didn't let on. "I'm a little surprised, though, that today's ceremony merits coverage like this."

"Well," said Rosa diplomatically, "I'm also here because I've heard so much about the complex and its history with the Dodgers, so I figured this was the perfect opportunity to check it out."

"Fantastic. I'll have you there in a second." She exited the airport and headed for the complex. "Mr. Hayward, have you ever been here before?" she asked as they rolled along.

"Please call me Darnell," he replied. "And yes, I've been here once before, specifically 2012. My senior year in high school our team came down here for Spring Training. It was called Historic Dodgertown then."

"Oh, yes. We just made the official name change last year when MLB took control of the complex. Since you've been here there have been a few changes, including the building we're dedicating today, but you're also going to recognize a lot of the same places from 2012."

"I'm sure I will," he replied as they entered the familiar gate that led to the registration building and the villas beyond it.

"Can I get you guys some lunch?" asked Brandi. "We've got a good hour and change until the ceremony."

"No, we're fine," said Darnell, looking around and smiling at the surrounding structures. "Tell you what, though. Could Rosa and I borrow a golf cart and take a spin around the complex? I'd like to show her the sights… and to see how much I remember."

"Kind of a trip down memory lane?" said the girl, echoing Rosa's earlier comments.

"Yeah, something like that. Just hold onto our bags till then, okay?"

"Sure thing. Just give me a second." She parked outside the registration building, went inside, and shortly emerged with a couple of water bottles and the key to one of a row of utility carts that were used by the complex staff. "Here you go," she said, tossing it to Darnell. "Use cart number two over there. Just make sure you're at the indoor building by 3 PM. It's located where the tennis courts and basketball courts used to be. Do you remember where that is?"

"Sure," he said.

"And if you finish your touring early, Rhonda and I will be in the administrative offices near Holman Stadium, getting things ready. Have fun!" She started the car and headed over to the other side of the complex.

"So here we are," said Rosa, swigging some water. "The Jackie Robinson Training Complex."

"Yup. But to me it's still Dodgertown," said Darnell. "Let's go for a ride." He removed his suit jacket and draped it over his seat back. They climbed into the cart and started it up.

"Here are the villas we stayed in," said Darnell, beginning the tour. "Paco and I were in #14. We thought we were real bigshots, let me tell you." They rolled past the conference center, the practice mounds, and the indoor batting cages nearby. "God, it looks the same," he marveled. "So many memories." They wove their way around the practice diamonds and passed the pitching wall as well, its red strike zone square a bit faded with the passage of time. The palm trees lining the cart paths stood motionless in the stifling heat, and Rosa started fanning herself with a tissue from her handbag.

"Where's the stadium?" she asked. "There must be an area there where we can get out of the sun."

"We're on our way," he replied, and pointed the cart towards the footbridge that connected the two sides of the complex.

"So this is the famous bridge," she said as they approached. "I can see what you meant about being like a jungle underneath it. You wouldn't catch me down there, even in daytime."

"Me neither." But still, he stopped the golf cart and set the brake, taking in the scenery.

"More memories?" she said.

"Yeah," he replied. "But it's different at night."

"I would imagine."

They crossed the bridge and turned left on Duke Snider Drive, coming to a stop at the designated spectator entrance to Holman Stadium, which was situated behind home plate. "When I went that night with the Dodgers, we entered down the right field line, as I remember," he said.

"Uh-huh," she replied blandly.

They climbed the steps to the concession area and press box, where Darnell pointed out the stadium's dedication plaque from 1953. "Let's sit here for a bit," said Rosa. "It's out of the sun, and we have a nice view of the field." Indeed, on this sultry summer day the deserted ballpark's panoramic views were like an old-time postcard. Darnell pointed to the new complex logo on the scoreboard in left center and noted that more modern green box seats had replaced the ones he remembered from 2012. He also reminded Rosa of the grassy berm beyond the outfield fence. The newly renovated administration offices were visible beyond the right field enclosure.

"It's a beautiful park," she observed. "Very quaint."

"You got that right," he said, sipping from his bottle. "I loved playing here that time against Vero Beach. And, of course, the time before with the Dodgers." He paused. "You still don't believe me, do you?" he said.

"Let's just say I'm thinking about it," she replied.

"Fair enough."

She looked at her watch. "We've got some time to kill," she said, pulling out her tape recorder. "You've told me all about what happened to you after you got back to Kansas City, and your baseball career, etc., but you haven't mentioned your grandfather. So what happened with all that?"

Darnell looked at her and smiled, but it was a smile tinged with sadness. He said, "I got home to Kansas City, which of course was rainy and still pretty cold. Of course, everybody wanted to hear all about Vero Beach and our Spring Training trip. So we sat down in the living room and I told Mom and Dad and my grandfather how I'd done a complete turnaround down there, how my wildness had left me, and how I'd posted a standout performance against Vero Beach. Now, I didn't mention the nighttime stuff because it was too crazy. But the whole time I was telling the story, I caught my grandfather looking at me with this kind of knowing smile. And I figured I'd wait a little while, at least, before bringing it up with him."

"Did you tell him you'd met Charlie Sutton?"

"That was another thing I felt uncomfortable about bringing up," he replied. "So again, I left it hanging out there. That must sound stupid to you, but I was seventeen."

"So you and your grandfather never talked about what really happened to you?"

"Oh, no, we did. It took another couple months. Like I said, I had a really good senior season. So one day I came home from school and my grandfather was sitting at the kitchen table, reading about my start the day before, where I struck out ten guys or something like that. I poured myself a glass of milk and sat across the table from him.

"Nice game yesterday," he began. "Looks like you had your stuff workin'."

"No doubt," I said.

Then he said, "Seems like you figured it all out in Vero."

At that point I decided to take a chance. "PawPaw," I said, "you know what happened to me down there, don't you?"

"With what?"

"With the Dodgers, PawPaw," I said. "The *Brooklyn* Dodgers. You *know*."

He grinned a little. "Well, let's just say I have an idea," he said. "Now, you fill me in."

"You're gonna think it's crazy."

He said, "Maybe not."

"Okay then," I said, "here's what I remember." And I went through the whole story, from my first meeting with "Ed," then "Harold;" Joe's pitching lessons; and finally, Jackie and Campy, and our final workout at Holman Stadium.

He listened with a sense of wonder and amazement—but never disbelief. "And you say the guys would work with you in the dead of night, but it was bright enough to see?"

"Yeah," I said. "I couldn't figure it out."

"Hmm," he said. "And you didn't let on about this to your teammates and coaches?"

"No," I said. "And I had my chances, especially with my catcher, Paco Gonzales, but I was sure they wouldn't understand. Truth be told, a lot of the guys thought I was a head case; they felt that was why I'd developed the wildness in the first place."

"I see."

"But here's another thing, PawPaw," I said, "something that hit me from the get-go. All the Dodgers called me *Willie*. They thought I was *you*. Why is that?"

He sighed and looked past me out the window to our backyard. "Well, son, to answer your question, I guess I have to go way back to the beginning. It's a story I should have told you a long time ago, but I never saw the need.

"To start, my grandparents were slaves in Mississippi. After the Civil War, my grandfather became a sharecropper, but that wasn't much better of an existence. So, after my parents married, they came to Kansas City in the 1920s during the time when many colored folks migrated north because there were no opportunities for work in the deep South. We lived in a Black section of the city. It was Mom, Dad, me, and my late sister Jenny.

"As a kid, I played a lot of sandlot ball, nothing organized like they have today. Me and my friends played from sunup to sundown. We just chose up sides and *played*. My father, who worked in a meatpacking factory, didn't have much, but since I was the only son, he scraped together the money to buy me things I needed to play ball, like a glove and bat. When the glove got a hole in it I patched it up, and I used to hammer small nails into the bat whenever it cracked to hold it together. A new baseball was a prized possession, and me and my friends wrapped ours up with friction tape after they started to unravel. You've heard the phrase 'tear the cover off the ball'? Well, we used to do it all the time." He chuckled at the memory.

"Right away, I showed ability as a pitcher. I could always throw hard. Unfortunately, there was nobody to notice. Even when I attended Lincoln High School—which was all Black, because the Kansas City schools were all segregated—we could only play intramurals, because there were no other colored high schools around, and the white schools wouldn't play us.

"Well, during the spring of my senior year I heard about an open tryout the Monarchs were having at Muehlebach Stadium, where the Kansas City Athletics used to play before they moved to Oakland. So I went and did well, and they signed me. I started games and I relieved, too. Our manager, Buck O'Neil, a great man, brought me along slowly. Now, at that time the Negro Leagues were beginning to decline, what with Jackie Robinson being signed in '46 and other great players following soon after. But the Monarchs were still a first-class club, talent- wise. They sent many great players to the big leagues besides Jackie, like Satchel Paige, Ernie Banks, and Elston Howard, the first Negro to play for the Yankees.

"Life with the Monarchs was tough, but exciting. I got to travel around to the other cities in the Negro

American League, even though it was by bus, not the fancy jet planes they use today. The trips were long and hot; you could play a doubleheader one day, drive all night, and play in another city the next afternoon, wearing the same dirty uniforms. We ate a lot of roadside burgers and greasy fries. But I was young and didn't know any better. I was making a few dollars, and there was some status in Kansas City if you were a pro ballplayer, even if it wasn't the big leagues.

"Anyway, we won the NAL West Division title in 1950 and the half-season pennant in 1951. But by the '52 season I was aiming higher. So I went to Mr. O'Neil and asked if he would recommend me to the Dodgers. His opinion was really respected, even in white baseball, so the Dodgers told me to come down to Vero Beach for Spring Training in 1953 and they would give me a look. They didn't promise anything, but I was pretty confident I could make it. I had to be, because I was gambling my Monarchs salary on it. So, the Monarchs gave me my release and wished me luck.

"When I got down to Vero Beach, I was pretty scared. I didn't expect that there would be *hundreds* of players there. I felt like I was just a number. And I was assigned to a barracks with all white boys, which I'd never experienced, either in school, or of course, in the Negro Leagues. So that kind of put me on edge, even though my barracks mates were fairly polite to me. I got the feeling this was a new experience for them, too.

"Anyway, all of this stuff was swirling around in my head, and it led me to being wild with my control. I was trying too hard, aiming the ball instead of just throwing it, like I had with the Monarchs.

"So the Dodgers had this practice area called 'the

strings,' which Branch Rickey had thought up, kind of a strike zone adjuster for the pitchers. You'd throw off a mound and all, but you had to keep your pitches inside the strings. Well, that got me even more flustered, and I started throwin' the ball all over the place."

"I know the feeling," I said.

"Then one day, a bunch of the Brooklyn guys were passing by our minor league workout, and Duke Snider stopped to watch. Pee Wee, too. Why I caught their eye, I don't know. Maybe it's because my catcher was diving all over the place, cursing his head off. And maybe it's because I was the only colored pitcher there. Or maybe both. So then, Pee Wee called Joe Black over, and Jackie and Roy followed him. Joe watched me throw a few and said, "Willie, you're all fouled up." And right then, they started working with me. For the next couple weeks, they took time from their own training schedule to seek me out. Sometimes it was the physical stuff, what you guys call 'mechanics' today, but it was also to give me pep talks and keep my spirits up, that sort of thing. And it made all the difference.

"Near the end of camp, when the big club was getting ready to head north, those guys gave me a serious talking-to about staying on the straight and narrow and keeping my eye on my goal of making it to the Majors. It just didn't work out."

I said, "I know, PawPaw. Charlie Sutton told me."

"*Sutton!*" He blurted. "*Charlie* Sutton? He's still alive?"

"Yessir," I said. "The guy who runs Dodgertown heard I was interested in the history of the place, and he arranged for me to meet with Charlie. He told me what happened, PawPaw." Man, it was killing me to say this to him. His eyes got all teary, and he had to take out a handkerchief and wipe them.

"Charlie had me over to his house in Gifford," I said. "He's lived there for years. His wife Mae is really nice, too. Paw Paw, his whole living room is covered with photos of the Dodgers, and he has these crazy cool scrapbooks, too. He worked at Dodgertown for well over fifty years."

My grandfather just sat there, staring at me. So, I decided to go ahead. "Charlie told me about that Saturday night in Gifford. About how he had too much to drink, and you stood up for him when some guy got in his face for talking to his girl."

"That's what he told you?"

"Yeah, why?"

"Because it was the other way around, son," he said. "*I* was the one who'd had too many, and I was talking big and all that, showing off for that girl. And her boyfriend, this big ornery guy, came over, and Charlie tried to cool things down, but the guy wasn't having it, and a brawl started. And me, the big man, almost got his pitching arm tore out of the socket. As for Charlie, he nearly lost his job over it. So it was all my fault for talking him into taking me there."

"Well, he blames himself, seems like," I said, and forged ahead. "Why did you make him believe you had died, PawPaw?"

He closed his eyes for a moment. "Oh, Lord," he said. "I know it was stupid. I was so embarrassed I just wanted to go home and disappear. I didn't want any of the guys, especially Jackie, to know how dumb I'd been, how I hadn't listened to them. It's the same reason I never told you. Who wants to learn his grandfather was a failure? So I got a job here in Kansas City with the rec department, settled down with your grandmother, and closed the door on that part of my life."

"Would you want to reconnect with Charlie?" I asked, knowing full well I'd given Charlie our phone number in Kansas City.

"I'd have to study on that a while," he said.

"There's one thing that I'm still not getting, though," I pressed. "It seems like what happened to me down there in Dodgertown kind of mirrors what you experienced. How could that possibly be?"

Again, he teared up, but not as bad as the first time. "Listen," he said. "When you get as old as me you start to wonder about things, question things. And some stuff you don't talk about, not even to your own daughter—or her husband, who might think you're going 'round the bend mentally. But I'll tell you this Darnell, because of what you experienced:

"I knew something was gonna happen to you down there. Exactly *what*, I wasn't sure. The thing is, son, those guys, those Dodgers, they come to me in my dreams. Have been for a while. And I told 'em all about you, and how you needed help, and they listened. So, I guess they just took it from there, because that's what the Brooklyn Dodgers were all about."

* * *

Rosa pushed the OFF button on her tape recorder and put it away. "You know," she said, "if you consider your career and your grandfather's, they *did* follow a similar path. You're both pitchers, right? Both of you were considered to have lots of potential, but you developed control problems. And then, both of you had a life-changing experience in Dodgertown that sent you in a different direction.

"Like your grandfather, you began your pro career with a Kansas City team. For him, it was the Monarchs; and for you, the Royals. Unfortunately, he never reached his goal of making it to the Dodgers, but you made it there, Darnell. He must be very proud of you."

"Well, he was," said Hayward.

"Was?"

"He died the day after I signed, Rosa."

Chapter Sixteen

There was a modest group of dignitaries who had already assembled inside the new indoor facility by the time Darnell and Rosa pulled up in the golf cart. "I hope this place is air-conditioned," she said as they hustled toward the entrance, Darnell putting on his dress jacket.

Once inside, they were introduced by Brandi to Rhonda Medeiros, the complex director, and the mayor of Vero Beach, who was on hand for the photo op. The opening was being covered by the *Press Journal,* Vero's local paper, and the regional TV news channel had a reporter and cameraman on hand as well. Major League Baseball had sent an emissary from the front office, as Commissioner Rob Manfred was in Colorado for the All-Star Game festivities. There were also some local high school and college baseball and softball coaches present, and an entire Little League team, in uniform, who gaped at the cavernous building.

While they were waiting, Darnell did a couple quick interviews with the media, telling them about his first visit to the complex as a highschooler and providing suitable soundbites for the evening news later that evening. He was just finishing up with the TV crew when he spied a trio of people quietly entering, and he broke into a smile. Joe Burgos, a little grayer and heavier than he recalled, was pushing a wheelchair that carried a frail Charlie Sutton, nattily dressed as usual. Mae, as always, was by his side, in a faded print dress.

Apparently, these were the people Rhonda had been waiting for to begin the ceremony, and she quickly instructed all attendees to be seated in the rows of folding chairs that had been set up in centerfield of the Astroturf indoor practice diamond. The Little League coach herded his squad into their seats, and Rhonda approached a portable podium that sported the logo of the Jackie Robinson Training Complex.

"Thank you all for coming out on this very warm Florida day," she began. "My name is Rhonda Medeiros, and I'm the Managing Director of the Jackie Robinson Training Complex. We are here today to officially open the Building 42 indoor training facility, and it is truly state-of-the-art. The building is 38,000 square feet and includes this half-turf field upon which we are sitting, four indoor batting cages, meeting rooms, and other amenities that will easily accommodate any athletic program, from youth league to the pros. It has won a 2021 Indian River County Industry Appreciation Award for architectural recognition. It is a welcome addition to our complex, which yearly plays host to a plethora of baseball and softball teams, tournaments, and MLB sponsored programs at every level of competition, as well as other sports such as soccer and lacrosse. I have no doubt that the addition of Building 42 will only enhance our already stellar reputation as a top-notch training facility here in Florida."

She then turned over the podium to the mayor, who spoke glowingly of the Robinson complex as a cornerstone of Vero Beach's tourist industry and a source of civic pride, going back to its original construction in the 1940s. As he spoke, Darnell's eyes wandered over to where Joe, Charlie and Mae sat, and he started to formulate what to say to these people whom he'd last had contact with when he was a high schooler.

After the mayor, the MLB representative said a few words and then gave the podium back to Rhonda, who said, "We are also honored to have a current member of the World Champion Los Angeles Dodgers with us today. Darnell Hayward has flown cross-country to participate in this gala event. Darnell, would you care to share a few thoughts?"

Medeiros's invitation took him a bit by surprise, but he felt Rosa nudging him in the ribs. "Get up there and say something," she whispered. So he stood and walked to the podium as cameras clicked and the crowd politely applauded—except for the Little Leaguers, who whooped it up, excited to have a Major Leaguer in their midst.

"Thank you," he began. "I'm not much at making speeches, so I'll keep this short. Besides, I see they've set up a table with sandwiches and cookies and cold drinks, and I haven't eaten in quite a while." The audience laughed, and he calmed down.

"I'm here representing the Dodgers because, as most of you know, it was the Dodgers—the *Brooklyn* Dodgers—who first established a training facility in Vero Beach, way back in 1948. The press nicknamed it Dodgertown, and the name stuck. It was a facility where their Major League club, and all the hopeful players of their minor league teams, hundreds of guys in all, came to train and sharpen their baseball skills under picturesque palm trees in the beautiful Florida sun. It wasn't much at first—a few stubbly fields and military barracks where the players slept—but it was a start, the first such facility of its kind."

He looked over at the Little Leaguers. "What you young players may not know, though, is that Dodgertown had another reason for being besides just the baseball aspect. You see, kids, back in the 1940s, and well afterwards, the state of Florida—including Vero Beach, the beautiful town you call home—was segregated. That means that African American people like me were not allowed to use public facilities like department stores or movie theaters or restaurants. It was hard for people with my skin color even to go to the *beach* in Vero Beach.

"And so, when Branch Rickey—the man who ran the Dodgers and signed Jackie Robinson, the first Black player in the Major Leagues in the 20th century—came up with the idea of a Spring Training facility in Florida, he constructed a place that would house *all* of the organization's players, Black, white, and Latino, with the same accommodations available to all. Dodgertown was a model community for the society that existed outside its gates; it's no accident, then, that during those years the Brooklyn Dodgers were the class of the National League. In fact, this place where you are today is the only sports facility in the United States listed as a historic site of the U.S. Civil Rights Trail, because it was a place where people in our society who cared about inclusion and equality challenged the institution of segregation to advance social justice.

"But for me, the Jackie Robinson Training Complex is more personal. You see, my grandfather, Willie Jackson, came here to try out for the Dodgers in 1953, after having played in what were called the Negro Leagues—the only leagues African American players like him could participate in prior to the Dodgers signing Jackie Robinson. And then, in 2012, when this place was known as Historic Dodgertown, I came here with my high school team from Kansas City for a week of Spring Training, and I can't tell you what it meant to my career." He paused and looked over at Rosa, who nodded in agreement. "That's why I've traveled all this way, to the place where it all began for me, and for so many others. And it's why I'm challenging all of you young players to find out all you can about the Brooklyn Dodgers, and Dodgertown, and how they set the example for the community which you enjoy living in today. Thank you."

The gathered people stood and applauded as Darnell made his way back to his seat, offering high-fives to the Little Leaguers as he passed by. "I thought you didn't like making speeches," chided Rosa as he sat down.

"Was it good?" he asked hopefully.

"No," she replied, "it was *perfect*."

After Rhonda closed the ceremony and invited everyone to enjoy the luncheon spread that had been set out, Darnell busied himself giving autographs to his new fans, signing everything from baseballs to hats and tee shirts. One young man even had him autograph his arm. But although the visiting dignitaries and coaches also sought his attention, there were three people he just had to visit with, and he headed over.

"That was some speech," said Joe Burgos, administering a bear hug. "You've sure filled out since high school, Darnell."

"So have you," joked the pitcher. "What are you up to now, Joe?"

"Well," he explained, "when the Dodgers left Vero for Arizona, the town temporarily took over the complex, and I figured it was time to move on. So, I got a job with the Miami Marlins, who as you know train south of here in Jupiter. I now run their Spring Training operation. By the way, do you remember our trainer, Amanda Lisnow? She's now the head trainer for a team in the WNBA. I still keep in touch with our staff from Historic Dodgertown. Those were great years. And who is this with you?"

"Rosa Santos from *El Comentario* in LA," she said, extending her hand. "I came down to cover the event."

"Hope you're enjoying this little slice of baseball heaven," said Joe.

"Oh, I am," she replied, and they proceeded to make small talk.

Meanwhile, Darnell approached Charlie, who sat quietly in his wheelchair, sipping some lemonade while Mae nibbled on a sandwich. "How's the lemonade, Mr. Sutton?" he asked. "As good as Mrs. Sutton's?"

"Nah, too sweet," he replied. "How you doing, son?"

"Not too bad. I'm so glad to see the both of you again."

"It's been a while, that's for sure," said Mae. "You're all grown up, and a big leaguer, too!"

"Yes, ma'am. But I still remember the hospitality you showed me when you had me over for dinner that one night. It meant a lot to me. The whole trip did."

"That makes me happy," said Charlie. "We had us a good conversation, as I recall."

"Yessir." Darnell got down on one knee and looked into the old man's eyes, which were staring straight ahead. It was then he realized Charlie had lost his sight since they'd last met. "Mr. Sutton," he said softly, "did you ever speak to my grandfather again?"

"What?" the old man asked. "You mean he didn't tell you?"

"Uh, no, sir. I mean, when I got home I told him about seeing you, and that you knew he wasn't really dead, but that was about it."

"Well now," he said, "that sounds like Willie. But let me tell you what happened. I called your house one day, maybe a few months after you and I talked, and he picked up. I said, 'I can't believe I'm talking to a dead man!' and Willie managed to laugh about it, which broke the ice.

"So we talked and talked. Seemed like hours went by before we said goodbye. Willie filled me in on what he'd been doing since '53, and I did the same. And he apologized for cutting me out of his life all those years; said he felt like a fool after what he'd done that night in Gifford, that he didn't want to face anybody. But I told him not to worry about it. Once we got that out of the way we chatted regularly, especially after he had your parents buy him his own cell phone and he figured out how to use it."

Darnell laughed. "Yeah, I remember him getting it for Christmas and wondering what the heck he needed a cell phone for."

"Well, it was for me. I don't think he wanted to tie up your home phone with our chats. And to keep them private, I guess."

"Speaking of which, I want to thank you for changing the story about that night at *Smokey's* so that you looked like the guy to blame. My grandfather told me the real deal when we finally spoke about it."

"I see. Well, I just didn't want to say anything that would tarnish his image for you. And it really was me who got punched out by that woman's boyfriend. I still have a chipped tooth as a souvenir."

Darnell couldn't help but laugh. "So, what did you guys talk about?" he asked.

"Well, baseball, of course. But mostly about you. He was so proud of you, son. We followed your career through college, the minors, and the Royals. And when you signed with the Dodgers, he was so thrilled…" Charlie's voice trailed off and his sightless eyes got watery.

"Hey now, Charlie Sutton, there'll be none of that," said Mae, dabbing the old man's tears with her napkin. "This is a happy occasion, remember?"

"You're right, Mama," he replied. "Someday I'll see Willie again, God willing. And all the other guys, too."

"Amen," said Darnell.

Chapter Seventeen

By the time the last cookie had been devoured and all the goodbyes had been said, it was close to 4 PM. But of course, Darnell's day wasn't over, because his newest fans were pleading for a little more of his time. So, he had the staff rustle him up a bag of balls, a glove, and a bat, and he did a mini-clinic on baseball fundamentals with the kids, the sleeves of his dress shirt rolled up to the elbows. Rosa stood to the side, sipping sweet tea with Rhonda and Brandi and taking it all in. Finally, the coaches told the kids it was time to go, and they all high-fived their new hero on the way out.

"That was fun," said Darnell, waving goodbye as the youngsters trooped towards the exit.

"Thanks so much for hanging around," said Rhonda. "I'm sure the Little Leaguers were thrilled to interact with you."

"No problem," he joked, "it's my throwing day anyway."

"So," said Brandi, "are you guys leaving right away or staying over? If the Dodgers haven't found you accommodations, we have a couple of the villas available. The others are booked for a week-long tournament that's beginning tomorrow."

Darnell looked at Rosa. "It's your call," he said.

"I don't know if I'm up for another long plane ride today," she confessed. "We can head out tomorrow."

"Great," he said, a sense of relief in his voice. "I'll call the hotel in Vero and cancel our reservations there. It'll be cool to stay in the villas again."

The group hopped into Brandi's SUV and drove to the administrative building, where Darnell and Rosa picked up their travel bags. After a heartfelt thanks and goodbye from Rhonda, Brandi took them over to the villas, where she handed each a key. "These rooms are both doubles, so you'll have a lot of space to stretch out," she said. "What are you doing for dinner? Do you need help with that?"

"No worries," said Hayward. "We can figure that out. We would appreciate a ride to the airport tomorrow morning, though. Say, about 9 AM?"

"I'll be here," promised the young lady, and left them alone.

"You hungry?" he said.

"Yeah," she confessed. "I was so busy talking to Joe Burgos and a couple other people that I hardly had a bite."

"Me too. How about we meet out front here at seven and go get something to eat. I'll call for an UBER. Sound good?"

* * *

After a welcome hour and change off their feet in the air-conditioned rooms, Darnell and Rosa reconvened on the pavement of Jackie Robinson Avenue. It was twilight, and the baseball globe streetlights had just been turned on. A light breeze had mercifully kicked up.

"Did you rest at all?" Rosa asked.

"Oh yeah. Checked in with my wife and daughter, too, and told them I'd be home tomorrow. You?"

"I managed to nod off for a bit, and also called my editor. He said to take tomorrow off, and the day after that as well."

"Sweet," said Hayward as the UBER rolled through the entrance and passed the registration building. "There's our ride."

"So, where are we going?" she inquired as they climbed in.

"Someplace appropriate for this trip," he replied. "I think you'll like it."

* * *

As the UBER made its way east past Royal Palm Pointe and turned right onto the bridge, Rosa took in the view of the Indian River Inlet below. Fishing skiffs and sailboats crisscrossed its cobalt blue waters, and a large American flag flapped in the breeze in Veterans Park on the other side. "It's beautiful," she said. "I know I'm used to the Pacific Coast, but there's something to be said for this area as well."

"My feelings exactly. I remember the first time I came over this bridge, and then ended up seeing the Atlantic Ocean for the first time. It blew me away. Plus, the water's warmer!"

"You think I'm underdressed?" she asked as they sped towards the intersection of A1A. "This outfit was all I brought."

"You're fine," he said. "I'm just happy I brought this golf shirt in my travel bag. The dress shirt got a little sweaty during my clinic with the kids."

"That was nice of you to do, Darnell," she said. "You didn't have to."

"I know," he replied. "But when I looked at those kids, and saw they were a pretty diverse group, I couldn't help thinking about how far Vero Beach has come since my grandfather was here. It just made me happy, so I figured, why not?"

"A lot of guys in the Majors would've wanted an appearance fee for what you did today," she stated. "But not you. How come?"

"Like I said, it was something I had to do. Besides, I'm telling you a story, right? It was important for us to come here."

She shrugged. "If you say so."

Minutes later they turned left onto Ocean Drive and came to a stop in front of a restaurant that occupied the bottom floor of a beachside resort. A bright green and white awning shaded the entrance, and the scripted name *Bobby's* adorned the light gray shiplap façade next to it.

Rosa stepped out of the car as Darnell handed the driver an additional generous tip, asking him to return in a couple hours for a ride back to Dodgertown. "Doesn't look too fancy," she observed.

"It's not meant to be. But I think you'll enjoy it."

They stepped inside the legendary restaurant/lounge which was fairly lively, despite it being a Monday. In deference to the Covid-19 pandemic the smaller tables had been spaced out a bit, but since Florida's Covid spacing policies were pretty lax, the rectangular bar was populated with patrons. But the main attraction of *Bobby's*, despite its reputation for good food and drink, was the wealth of sports memorabilia that covered its walls, with everything from autographed photos, bats and balls, to framed jerseys and historic sports documents. Of course, much of what was on display was related to the Los Angeles Dodgers, who had made *Bobby's* their go-to hangout during Spring Training for many seasons. However, unlike other sports bars that both Darnell and Rosa had frequented over the years, the vibe here was more laid-back and local. Perhaps this was because the clientele was decidedly more middle-aged. The two of them didn't exactly feel out of place there because of their comparative youth, but heads did turn when they entered.

"It's like reruns of *Cheers*, only in Florida," observed an amused Rosa.

The other thing that got them noticed was that at the very moment they entered the bar area (there was also a healthy crowd on the outside patio), Hayward's face was flashing on one of the many overhead TVs, which was tuned into the evening news. People in the bar were glancing at the footage of him giving his speech, then at him, and then back at the screen. "You're busted," said Rosa as they slid into an empty booth near a glass case displaying autographed baseballs from Sandy Koufax and Don Drysdale, the Dodgers' pitching greats of the 1960s.

It didn't take long for the buzz to get around the bar that a pro ballplayer was in their midst, and they had barely started examining their menus when an older gent stopped by and identified himself as the owner. "Bobby McCarthy," he said, shaking first Rosa's and then Darnell's hand. "What brings you two to Vero?"

"Well, Darnell was invited to the dedication of a building at the Jackie Robinson Training Complex," explained Rosa, "and I'm covering it for my newspaper back in LA."

"You're Rosa Santos," said the affable owner. "I've seen you on TV over the past year. Sorry for your troubles, Miss."

"No worries," she replied. "It's in the past. So tell me about your place here."

"I'm originally from Long Island, New York," he explained, "but I wanted to get out of the cold. So, I came down here and opened *Bobby's* in 1981. We cultivated a relationship with the team when they came to train in Dodgertown, and of course the locals got wind of it and started showing up to mingle with the pros. Tommy Lasorda, the Dodgers' longtime manager, was a regular, and Terry Collins, who was a minor league skipper for them and later managed the Mets, became a close friend.

"We also get pro golfers and other celebrities, such as the novelist Carl Hiaasen. But the good thing is, our patrons know to leave these people alone and let them enjoy their meal, kind of what they're doing right now with you."

"It's much appreciated," said Hayward, who many times, especially when he was with the Royals, had a family dinner outing interrupted by autograph-seeking fans, though he always tried to be accommodating.

"If I might ask," said McCarthy, "how did you hear about this place? The Dodgers have been gone from Vero for years."

"Actually," said Darnell, "way back when I was in high school, my team came down to Dodgertown for Spring Training, and I met a guy named Charlie Sutton, who mentioned *Bobby's*. I never forgot the name."

"Charlie Sutton!" cried McCarthy. "I haven't seen him or his wife in a few years. He was an institution at Dodgertown. Such nice people. Do you know how they're doing?"

"We saw them today, actually," said Rosa. "At the ceremony. They're getting on in years, but they seem to be doing okay. Right, Darnell?"

"You know it," he agreed. "So, what do you recommend for tonight?"

McCarthy touted their prime rib loin and Danish baby back ribs, which sounded great to the famished visitors, and they took him up on it. As they waited for their meals, their host sent over a bottle of wine, and their server, a veteran named Julie, poured them each a glass.

"Do you feel funny when people recognize you from the scandal stuff?" asked Hayward. "I mean, you handled it well just now, but it has to bother you."

"It's not as bad as it was last year," she replied quietly. "But it was all over TV and the newspapers. First, it became a big deal locally; but then ESPN and CNN got all over it, and it went viral. I received all kinds of mail, some of it positive, and some really hateful and vile. Truthfully, I almost quit over it."

"I'm glad you didn't," he said. "You're a good writer."

"A good *female* writer," she said. "And that's what's made it tough. There is still, and always will be, a double standard for women in the sports media, Darnell. But let's move onto something else, or I won't enjoy my dinner."

"Such as?"

"I saw you talking to Charlie Sutton and I have to know, did he and your grandfather ever speak again?"

Hayward took a sip of wine and chuckled. "Oh, yeah, and quite frequently, it seems. So, I guess they patched things up okay."

"And it did your grandfather ever mention the whole Dodgertown ghost thing to Charlie?"

"Not that I can tell… he probably would've said a word to me about it today. In the end, it was something private between my grandfather and me."

Their dinners arrived on steaming platters, and they started eating. The ribs, which were covered with some kind of seasoning rub, were fall-off-the-bone tender; and the prime rib, topped with a tangy *au jus*, barely needed a knife to cut it. They ended up sharing their meals, which included a stuffed baked potato and creamy coleslaw.

"I'm gonna have to diet for the next week to make up for this," said Rosa, pausing briefly for a sip of wine. "This is definitely not your typical sports bar."

"You got that right," agreed Darnell, who was trying not to cover his fingers in barbecue sauce.

Rosa asked him if he was happy with his first season in Los Angeles so far. "You know it," he replied. "Skip uses me when he sees fit, and our team's humming along. But I think it's going to be a dogfight all year with the Giants. They were supposed to finish back in the pack, but we just can't shake them. We might have to acquire another starting pitcher to get us over the hump."

Rosa looked up. "You're on TV again," she giggled.

Hayward shook his head. "They must be replaying the local news every half hour. The price of fame," he said with a chuckle.

They finished as much of their meal as they could handle and were thus surprised and delighted when McCarthy sent over a massive dessert called Turtle Fudge Ice Cream Pie. "It's the house specialty," said Julie. So, they ordered coffee and started in on the frozen concoction.

"There is something that's bothering me, Rosa," said Darnell, keeping his mouthfuls small to avoid a case of brain freeze. "I've told you my whole story. I brought you down here to show you where it happened. And today you even met some of the people who were involved. But I can tell that you still don't believe me, not completely."

"What's important, Darnell, is that *you* believe it," she said diplomatically. "I wouldn't get too worked up about it."

"No," he said adamantly as the coffee arrived, "it *does* matter that you believe. What would it take to make that happen?"

"Listen," she said. "What you've told me is a great story. But take it from me, as someone who's had to deal with the subjects of truth and evidence for the past year, what I've been given from you is hearsay. It's your word only, with no corroborating evidence. Sorry, I wish there was something more solid you could provide for me to go on."

"Okay," he said. "Let me ask you a question, then."

"Go ahead," she said, lifting a huge spoonful of ice cream pie to her lips.

"What do I do every time I take the mound, just before I throw my first pitch?"

"Your little ritual. You get hold of that peace medallion around your neck, the one you've got on now, and you kiss it, and look up and say something to yourself before you put it away."

"You're very observant."

"Well, I'm a journalist. That's what I do."

"Do you know what I say to myself?"

"That quote that Jackie Robinson supposedly gave you?"

"Exactly. 'Pressure is a privilege.' And thanks for

proving you were actually paying attention. So, then you must also remember how Joe Black was asking me about what the peace medallion was."

"Uh-huh. You told him your girlfriend made it for you."

"Right. Then how do you explain *this*?" He reached into his jacket, which was draped over the back of his chair, and pulled out what seemed to be a photo of some sort. He slid it across the table and waited.

Rosa examined the yellowed black and white Kodak print with April 53 in embossed on its white border. The photo featured six men, five of them in creamy white Dodger uniforms with the letter B on their hats. Three of the Dodgers were Black men, and two were white. They stood side-by-side, their arms slung over each other's shoulders in a show of camaraderie. And in the middle of the group was a younger African American man clad in a baseball undershirt. And though he was not as recognizable, perhaps, as the Dodger teammates, two things stood out about the young Black man. The first was his dazzling smile, which contrasted sharply with his dark skin. The other was the peace medallion which hung from a cord around his neck.

Rosa's mouth fell open, and her spoon hit the table with a *thunk*. "This *can't* be," she managed. "Who's that with the Dodgers? Your grandfather… or *you*?"

"You tell *me*, Rosa," he said, his eyes burning intensely.

The journalist reached for her coffee cup, and Darnell could detect a tremor in her hand. She took a sip and looked into his eyes. "Ask for the check, will you?" she said. "We have to get back to Dodgertown."

Chapter Eighteen

The UBER ride back to the complex was a quiet one, and Darnell reflected on what had happened back at *Bobby's*. Outside of a reserved thank you when he'd quickly pulled out his wallet and left the server a $100 tip to cover McCarthy's "on the house" meal, Rosa had hardly said a word.

It was dark now, and the streets of Vero Beach were mostly deserted at this hour. The breeze had intensified, and rain was forecast for the following day. But the moon was still playing hide and seek from behind the swiftly moving clouds, and the oppressive humidity from earlier in the day had dissipated.

They entered the gate near the huge Jackie Robinson Training Complex sign that featured his famous #42, surrounded by a bed of tropical flowers and dwarf palms. The driver pulled up to the registration building where he'd picked them up hours earlier. Again, Darnell gave him a tip on top of the already paid-for fare; he thanked the ballplayer profusely and drove away, leaving the pitcher and the sportswriter by themselves.

"Let's walk," she said.

"Sure," he replied, and followed alongside. Soon they were on the cart path, and he knew where they were headed.

"You must've been a little scared, going out at night by yourself back then," she said finally. "I mean, not knowing what you would find, especially in the beginning."

"Yeah," he said, "it was strange, to say the least. But I just had to see where it was all going. It was like I was *supposed* to."

"It's hard to relate to for me," she said. "I've always been a concrete person, and I deal in facts and hard evidence."

"I get that."

They walked on.

"Do you believe in God, Rosa?" he asked. "Or that there's an afterlife?"

"Well," she said, "being from the Dominican, you know I had a Catholic upbringing. But I was never really into the whole organized religion thing. I believe that there's a higher *power* out there. If you want to call it God, that's fine. But the afterlife? I've never had cause to really consider it—that is, until you came along."

"Yeah, I know this is all a little bizarre."

They stepped onto the footbridge.

Rosa said, "You know, I've read about these places called portals which are supposed to be doorways from this world to the next. I guess for you, this bridge was one of those portals."

"Maybe so," he said with a shrug. "I really don't completely understand it myself. And I realize how difficult it could be for you—or anyone—to take it all in."

She managed a smile. "We sure spent a lot of time on this, didn't we? All of our clandestine coffee shop meetings, in a lot of different places. And I have cassette tapes and notebooks full of stuff to show for it. The thing is, Darnell, both you and I know that chances are this tale will never see the light of day. Nobody in their right mind would believe it. It's too far out."

"But… *you* believe it now, Rosa… don't you?"

"I guess us crazy people have to stick together," she said, and he breathed a sigh of relief. "Here's the thing, though," she continued. "You have to know in your heart of hearts that this story can't go public, even after you've retired, unless you want the men in the white suits coming after you. So why take all the time and effort to share it with *me*?"

He went to the railing and peered into the jungle-like vegetation. "Rosa," he said, "I know you think that most ballplayers today are self-centered, pampered, entitled jerks. And there are more than enough guys out there who would prove you right on a daily basis. The thing is, I could tell you were losing your faith in the game itself, and all that's good about it, and it bothered me really bad."

He turned back to her, and even in the partial moonlight she could detect the tears in his eyes. He said, "Somehow, through my grandfather, I was chosen for this experience because somebody, somewhere, determined that I needed something to believe in. And that something turned out to be myself, and my place in baseball's continuum. And that's why I chose you. Because I wanted you to believe again in the good and realize that you still belong in the game, too."

"And I thought *I* was the wordsmith here," Rosa said, trying mightily to keep from crying herself. She took one last look around. "You know," she said, "I'll probably never come to this place again, but I'll never forget it."

"Me neither," he said.

"Okay then, we're done here. Let's go back. We've got another long flight tomorrow, and it's been quite a day. Just one thing more, Darnell."

"Yes?"

"Thanks for choosing me."

Epilogue

"So, how was your little Florida excursion?" said Felipe Rodriguez when Rosa breezed into his office two days later.

"Very hot," she replied, sinking into one of the tatty chairs that faced her editor's desk, "but worth it. I'm going to get a good human interest story out of it, I think. Darnell Hayward's an interesting guy. It turns out his grandfather played in the Negro Leagues back in the day, so there's that angle. Plus, I learned a lot about Dodger history… you know, in the Jackie Robinson era."

"Well," he said, "I'm happy for you, but I'm gonna have to jolt you back to reality. The Dodgers have put their domestic issue pitcher on indefinite leave, and women's rights groups are pressuring the club to release him. On top of that, a couple more players in the Majors have been suspended for PEDs, a bunch of pitchers cited for doctoring the baseball with sticky stuff are complaining that they're being unfairly targeted, TV ratings and attendance are down because of the pandemic, and did I mention that there's the threat of a player lockout this coming winter that's hanging over the whole sport? *Ay-yi-yi.*"

He set his elbows on the desk before him and buried his face in his hands for a few seconds. Then he looked up. "When I was a kid in Mexico," he lamented, "I fell in love with baseball. And you know why? Because in 1981 the Los Angeles Dodgers brought up this chubby Mexican kid named Fernando Valenzuela to bolster their pitching staff. And that chubby Mexican kid went on to have one of the great seasons in the history of baseball. He caused a sensation they called 'Fernandomania.' Of course, because he was one of *us*, people in my little town idolized him.

"That year, the Dodgers won the World Series over the Yankees, in large part because of him, and I started writing little stories about Valenzuela in my grade school notebook and tuning into Dodger games he was pitching whenever we could get reception on our cheap plastic radio. Of course, I played baseball all the time, all day long; even so, I realized that a Major League career wasn't in the cards for me. But then I figured I could do the next best thing: I could *write* about it! And with a lot of sacrifice and hard work, here I am forty years later. But instead of writing about the game itself, we have to deal with all this other stuff. And it pains me, Rosa, to have to send you, who have been through so much, out there to cover these kinds of negative stories. For that, I apologize."

"Hey, Boss, it's no big deal," she said with a wink. "I can hack it, don't worry."

He gave her a suspicious look. "Wasn't it you who not too long ago was thinking of chucking the whole thing and forgetting about baseball altogether?"

"Yeah, you got me," she said. "I felt the same way as you do right now. But then it changed when somebody told me a story, which I'm now willing to share with you, and *only* you."

"Why?"

"Because you could use it."

The harried sports editor looked at his watch. "Is this a long story?"

"Yeah," said Rosa. "But it's a good one."

From the Author

I first visited Vero Beach in the early 2000s, when my parents were renting a condo in Vista Royale, a 55 and older community off US-1. It was February break from the school where I taught in Connecticut, and my family, which included my wife and daughter, were delighted to leave the frozen tundra of New England for warmer climes.

I had been to Florida before, mostly for college Spring Break vacations and the like, in places like Fort Lauderdale, where the whole town was transformed into a month-long frat party. But I learned very quickly that Vero Beach is most certainly *not* Fort Lauderdale—or Miami, or Jacksonville, or even Orlando. It has an ambience all its own, a more laid-back atmosphere conducive to relaxation away from the more populated areas. Of course, that made it a perfect fit for seniors like my parents, who were doing the Snowbird thing. So when they invited us down, I couldn't wait to once again enjoy the Florida sun and surf... and Spring Training baseball. Because Vero Beach was home to the famous Dodgertown, and I was in need of a baseball fix.

As a columnist for *Sports Collectors Digest,* whom I've been with since 1993, the prospect of doing a brief Spring Training tour and writing a feature about it was enticing. At the time, Dodgertown was centrally located in a row of MLB training outposts along Florida's East

Coast that included Jupiter (St. Louis Cardinals and Florida Marlins), Port St. Lucie (New York Mets), and Viera (Montréal Expos). Since all these venues were within a two-hour drive of each other, I figured I could spend a day at each and really enjoy them. And boy, did I. There's nothing better than hearing the crack of the bat and taking in the sweet smell of freshly cut grass while lounging under those swaying palm trees. So, while my wife and daughter were cadging autographs and such, I wandered the grounds of each site and took in its ambience.

All these places were pleasant facilities, busy with ballplayers going through drills and entertaining the many fans who came out to watch them. But Dodgertown was different. Since I was staying in Vero I started with it, and then went a second time before leaving for home. But truthfully, I could've spent the entire week there, and would have been very happy to do so.

Maybe it was because of the old-time feel of the grounds, with the cart path roads sporting names like Sandy Koufax Lane, Pee Wee Reese Boulevard and Duke Snider Drive, and those charming baseball globe streetlamps, complete with red stitching. Or perhaps it was the accessibility of the players and coaches, who were separated from the fans not by a tall chain-link fence as in the other Spring Training venues, but by a single waist-high yellow rope. There was clearly more interaction between the ballplayers and visitors here than in any of the other places I covered.

But most of all, Dodgertown had this sense of history, a hallowed ground kind of vibe that you couldn't escape once you remembered all the greats who had traversed those diamonds and their connecting paths. And where else but Holman Stadium could a visitor, at any time of day or night, just wander in, take a seat in the stands, and chill out for a while?

I was to visit Vero Beach and Dodgertown a few more times before the club left for Arizona after the 2008 season. The names of the managers and players changed during that last decade, but the welcoming atmosphere did not. Whether it was the "mayor" of Dodgertown, longtime player/manager/front office executive Tommy Lasorda holding court in his roving golf cart, guest coaches from the LA Dodgers' glorious past like Maury Wills supervising drills, or the everyday grounds crew and staff who greeted you with a smile and told you to have a nice day, Dodgertown never disappointed.

Of course, since the ballclub left (the LA logo is still featured in the wrought iron gates to Holman Stadium) the name of the complex has changed, from Dodgertown to the Vero Beach Sports Village to Historic Dodgertown (when my protagonist Darnell made his high school visit) and now the Jackie Robinson Training Complex as of 2020. But it's basically the same place.

I decided to write this book during my latest visit in the summer of 2021. I was now the proud owner of my own residence at Vista Royale and had been visiting yearly since we bought the place in 2013. The day I drove over, there was an MLB-sponsored program in progress named RBI Play Ball, which was aimed at minority high school level ballplayers. Such former luminaries as Ken Griffey Sr., Fred McGriff, Marquis Grissom and Jerry Manuel were working with young men under the brilliant sun on batting, fielding, and pitching techniques, and all the practice diamonds were being utilized. On another field past Holman Stadium, a women's soccer team was being put through their paces, reminding me that this complex, going back to when it was Dodgertown, has also played host to college and pro teams from all sports, including for a time the NFL New Orleans Saints.

I met with Rachelle Madrigal and Amanda Bracken, the real-life executives who help run this enormous operation, and told them about my book, and about my idea for the plot. "The footbridge is the key," I said. "I don't have a lot else figured out yet, but that will be the place where the action begins." These ladies were most helpful in providing information on the changeover in ownership from the Dodger organization to Major League Baseball and giving me an insight into how a normal day at the 80-acre complex works. And they wished me luck with the book.

On my way out, I couldn't help but stop on the footbridge one more time and take some photos, but even these images don't fully capture the feeling I've always gotten there. Whether it was watching the delight in my wife's eyes as she received autographs from current Dodgers manager Dave Roberts, who was then nearing the end of his playing career, or the famously named Milton Bradley, I couldn't help but think of all the Brooklyn and Los Angeles players who had paused there on their way to the locker room near Holman Stadium as they returned from a day on the practice diamonds, meeting and greeting their fans. And I thought, what better place for my protagonist to encounter some Dodger legends?

In closing, it is my hope that this book will prompt a visit to Vero Beach and the Jackie Robinson Training Complex for fans young and old. There are many great area restaurants to visit, including *Mulligan's* and

Bobby's from the book, and Vero's beach and boardwalk are a fine place to spend the day, not to mention the local golf courses, botanical gardens, and the like. And while the strip along US-1 is populated with virtually every fast-food restaurant, department store and pharmacy chain you can name, a couple minutes' ride away will take you back in time through the "old Florida" neighborhoods that still surround what was once—and still is—the crown jewel of Vero Beach: Dodgertown.

Acknowledgements

The time spent researching for this book was pure delight, as I am a baseball history fan at heart. Besides Rachelle Madrigal and Amanda Bracken, who helped me navigate the current Jackie Robinson Training Complex and its workings, there are a few books which have provided invaluable information about Dodgertown and "Dem Bums" that I invite you to read and enjoy: *The Rise and Fall of Dodgertown* by Rody Johnson, *Dodgertown* by Mark Langill, *Bums* by Peter Golenbock, and Roger Kahn's classic *The Boys of Summer*, which I first read in high school. There are also many Brooklyn Dodgers videos available on YouTube, especially those featuring Joe Black, that helped me flesh out his character, and the story of the 1953 Brooklyn club. I would be remiss if I did not mention two Facebook pages, and the wonderful friends I've made through them: **Jackie Robinson and Larry Doby USA**, and **Brooklyn Dodgers Nostalgia Society**. These groups are keeping alive the memory of the "Boys of Summer" for generations to come.

Special thanks go out to my stalwart proofreaders Herb Ross (who knows more about the Brooklyn Dodgers than anybody), and Barb Szepesi, my go-to grammar aficionado. And, as always, thanks to my sister Carol Young for her outstanding cover design.

Also, during the writing process, the following people lent their assistance and support: Martha Jo Black,

Jim Denny, Bobby McCarthy, Branch B. Rickey, Brent Shyer, Peter O'Malley, Vin Scully, and Carl Erskine. You helped make *The Kid from Dodgertown* come alive, and I'll be forever grateful.

The Golden Age of the Brooklyn Dodgers
A Brief History for Young Readers

The Brooklyn Dodgers entered the National League of Professional Baseball in 1884, though it would not be until 1947 that their "golden age" would begin. However, the team's early years, as well as the borough of New York City in which they played, would contribute to the legendary status that those Jackie Robinson teams would attain.

Brooklyn was considered a secondary community to Manhattan, which boasted the NL New York Giants, who played in the Polo grounds in Harlem. However, after 1921, they also had to contend with the Bronx's New York Yankees of the rival American League, and their star, Babe Ruth. Indeed, the Brooklyn club would cultivate intense rivalries with both of these franchises.

Brooklyn was an ethnically diverse borough in which the inhabitants developed their own distinctive dialect and pronunciations (example: Dodger pitcher Carl Erskine would be known as "Oisk"). The name "Dodgers" was itself indicative of the hardscrabble spirit of the borough, as it was derived from the reputed skill of Brooklyn residents in evading being struck by the local trolley streetcars. Their most famous home ballpark was Ebbets Field, a jewel opened in 1913 in the Flatbush section. It was dwarfed by the Giants' cavernous Polo Grounds and later, Yankee Stadium; but Brooklyn fans were fiercely proud of their ballpark and their ballclub. Unfortunately, they had little to show for it in their early years, when the team's name was even changed now and then, including such monikers as Bridegrooms, Superbas and Robins. Although the club did have a stretch of respectability in the World War I era, they sank into a malaise of mediocrity in the next two decades, which prompted the creation of the team's mascot by noted sports cartoonist Willard Mullin: a clownish hobo. Indeed, in Brooklynese, the ballplayers' fans lovingly referred to them as "Dem Bums." This identity would remain with the team as long as they were in Brooklyn, as the fans would develop a diehard loyalty to their ballclub that arguably has never been rivaled.

Despite a trip to the World Series in 1941 (the first of many losses to the Yankees), things would stay quiet for the Dodgers until 1946, when general manager Branch Rickey signed Jackie Robinson to a contract with the Dodgers' top farm team, the Montréal Royals. Rickey, who believed in integration, correctly anticipated the changes that were coming in America as thousands of Black soldiers, who had served bravely for their country, returned from the war seeking equality in the nation they had defended. Rickey was also aware, as were the other owners in Major League Baseball, that there was a vast untapped well of talent in the Negro Leagues; however, it was Rickey who was first willing to gamble upon signing Black players. Thus, with the approval of Commissioner "Happy" Chandler, the Dodgers led the way in the 20th century integration of baseball.

As noted in this novel, Robinson's signing was met with resistance, not only from the other owners who still refused to sign Blacks (the Yankees would not have one until Elston Howard in 1955, with the Boston Red Sox being the last in 1959); the players on opposing teams who attacked him either verbally or physically on the field with beanball pitches or spikes-high slides into second base as he attempted to turn a double play; or even some of his own teammates, who petitioned then-manager Leo Durocher to release Robinson during Spring Training in Havana, Cuba. However, Rickey and Durocher stood firm, and with the support of team captain Pee Wee Reese, and other players like Duke Snider and pitcher Ralph Branca, the uprising was put down. Thus, on opening day of 1947, the Golden Era of the Brooklyn Dodgers began.

During the eleven seasons Robinson was with the club, the Dodgers won the National League pennant in 1947 (with Robinson named Rookie of the Year), 1949, 1952, 1953, 1955, and 1956. Unfortunately, during these pennant-winning seasons the Dodgers' World Series opponent was the powerful Yankees, with superstars like Joe DiMaggio, Mickey Mantle and Whitey Ford. Alas, the famous cry of Brooklyn fans after each October defeat became "Wait till next year!" Mercifully, the Bums managed to break through in 1955, and the borough rejoiced.

The 1953 season, which is spotlighted in this novel, was representative of the Robinson era Dodgers. The ballclub won 105 games versus 49 losses, a single season club record that would stand until 2021 (with the regular season now extended from 154 to 162 games played). And yet, they would still fall to the Yankees in the World Series in six games. Roy Campanella would be named the National League Most Valuable Player, with Snider coming in third with a .336 batting average and 42 home runs. Right fielder Carl Furillo would win the National League batting championship, and first baseman Gil Hodges, just recently elected to the Baseball Hall of Fame in 2022, would post a solid .302 batting average with 31 homers.

During this era there developed a bond among the Dodger players—who included Blacks such as Campanella, Joe Black, Don Newcombe, and Jim Gilliam—as well as between the ballclub and their fans, that was unbreakable. There is no doubt that the creation of Dodgertown in 1948, which brought all the organization's players under one roof and contributed to the franchise's "us against the world" mentality so reflective of the borough in which they played, contributed to their success.

As history shows, Walter O'Malley, who had succeeded Rickey as managing partner, made the decision to move the franchise to the West Coast (he would be joined by the Dodgers' chief National League rivals, the Giants) after the 1957 season. This move, which is controversial even today, deeply affected the borough of Brooklyn, and those Bums fans who are still around lament the day their ballclub moved away. (The borough would not have a major professional team again until the Brooklyn Nets of the NBA in 2012). Only Snider and Reese from this book would make the move west, as Robinson would retire and Campanella would be tragically crippled in a car crash during the winter after the '57 season.

Of course, the Dodgers would go on to have great success in Los Angeles under the O'Malley family ownership. (Dodger Stadium, which is considered a classic ballpark of the modern era, was based architecturally upon Holman Stadium). They would continue to train in Vero Beach until 2008, even after the O'Malleys had sold the franchise some ten years earlier. Later on, Peter O'Malley would save Dodgertown when he took over the struggling "Vero Beach Sports Village" from the city and renamed it Historic Dodgertown, which it remained until 2019, when MLB assumed control and renamed it the Jackie Robinson Training Complex.

Thus, while the Dodgers have enjoyed much success on the field over many decades, the Jackie Robinson era Dodgers have achieved *immortality* for their excellence on the field and their role in the promotion of social change in America.

The Key Players

Although the Dodgers featured many ballplayers worthy of inclusion in any baseball book, here are the vital statistics of the characters from this novel from their tenure as Brooklyn/LA Dodgers. They are listed by uniform number.

Harold "Pee Wee" Reese #1
Tenure: 16 Seasons
Bats: Right Throws: Right
Position: Shortstop
Batting Average: .269
Home Runs: 126
Runs Batted In: 885
All-Star Game Appearances: 10
Elected to Baseball Hall of Fame: 1984

Edwin "Duke" Snider #4
Tenure: 16 Seasons
Bats: Left Throws: Right
Position: Centerfield
Batting Average: .300
Home Runs: 389
Runs Batted In: 1271
All-Star Game Appearances: 7
Elected to baseball Hall of Fame: 1980

Roy Campanella #39
Tenure: 10 Seasons
Bats: Right Throws: Right
Position: Catcher
Batting Average: .283
Home Runs: 260
Runs Batted In: 1017
All-Star Game Appearances: 11
National League Most Valuable Player: 1951, 1953, 1955
Elected to Baseball Hall of Fame: 1969

Jackie Robinson #42
Tenure: 11 Seasons
Bats: Right Throws: Right
Position: Second Base, Third Base, First Base
Batting Average: .313
Home Runs: 141
Runs Batted In: 761
All-Star Game Appearances: 7
National League Rookie of the Year: 1947
National League Batting Champion: 1949
National League Most Valuable Player: 1949
Elected to Baseball Hall of Fame: 1962

Joe Black #49
Tenure: 4 Seasons
Bats: Right Throws: Right
Wins: 22
Earned Run Average: 3.45
National League Rookie of the Year: 1952

About the Author

Paul Ferrante is originally from the Bronx and grew up in the town of Pelham, New York. He received his undergraduate and master's degrees from Iona College, where he was also a halfback on the Gaels' undefeated 1977 football team.

Paul was an award-winning secondary school English teacher and coach for over forty years, and the first recipient of the **Team Westport Community Leadership Award** for promoting cultural diversity within the school district.

He has also been a columnist for *Sports Collectors Digest* since 1993 on the subject of baseball ballpark history. Many of his works can be found in the archives of the National Baseball Hall of Fame in Cooperstown, New York. His writings have led to numerous radio, television, and podcast appearances related to baseball history.

The young adult **T.J. Jackson Mysteries** series has led Paul to speak at the 150th Anniversary Battlefield Commemoration in Gettysburg, Pennsylvania, the National Baseball Hall of Fame during their 75th Anniversary celebration, and the inaugural ParaConn paranormal convention in Connecticut in 2021. He has also been a guest speaker at many secondary schools and served as a presenter at the Westchester (NY) Young Writers High School Conference.

Paul's novel *30 Minutes in Memphis: A Beatles Story* has seen him interviewed on numerous podcasts around the world and favorably reviewed in various Rock n' Roll publications. He has also spoken at the annual Fest for Beatles Fans in New Jersey.

His novel *The Girl Who Stole J.E.B. Stuart* has been featured on numerous radio and podcast interviews and was the centerpiece in a **One Book - One Congregation** event for First Church Congregational in Fairfield, Connecticut as part of their **Racial Justice Pathway** program.

Paul lives in Stratford, Connecticut and Vero Beach, Florida with his wife Maria.

Please visit Paul's website www.paulferranteauthor.com for information on the **T.J. Jackson Mysteries** and his other writings; also visit the **T.J. Jackson Mysteries** page on Facebook.

www.ingramcontent.com/pod-product-compliance
Lightning Source LLC
Chambersburg PA
CBHW070343200726

48294CB00003B/763